DESIGN FOR LOVE

With her promotion to assistant art director at Market Media, a lovely new flat, and her handsome steady boyfriend Grant, Andrea Ross's future looks rosy. But when her gentle, fatherly boss decides to retire, and the company hires Luke Sullivan as the new art director, nothing is certain anymore. With a reputation as both a slave driver and a serial charmer of women, he quickly stamps his imprint on the department. Meanwhile, things with Grant aren't exactly going to plan . . .

GINNY SWART

DESIGN FOR LOVE

Complete and Unabridged

LINFORD
Leicester

First published in Great Britain in 2007

First Linford Edition
published 2019

A catalogue record for this book is available
from the British Library.

ISBN 978-1-4448-4068-1

Published by
F. A. Thorpe (Publishing)
Anstey, Leicestershire

Set by Words & Graphics Ltd.
Anstey, Leicestershire
Printed and bound in Great Britain by
T. J. International Ltd., Padstow, Cornwall

This book is printed on acid-free paper

A Bad Start!

'Oh horrors, look at the time,' muttered Andrea to herself as she hurried through to her tiny kitchenette to switch off the kettle. 'Too late for coffee; Grant will be parked down in the street by now, waiting for me.'

She opened the window and looked out to see if Grant's green sports car was double-parked outside her flat, its motor revving throatily as he waited impatiently for her.

But no, he wasn't there yet. Good.

She took in a deep breath of the cool, morning air, her heart lifting at the sight of the new green buds on the trees outside her window.

She was pleased with her decision to move across town to live closer to the park. The rent for this tiny flat cost more than her old digs but, with her promotion to assistant art director at

1

Market Media, she could just afford it.

Eventually, she meant to furnish the flat properly, but in the meantime she'd thrown a big Indian shawl over the sagging sofa and had bought a couple of colourful rugs to cover the old, threadbare carpet.

She took another deep breath and — with a mixture of excitement and dread — she thought about the day ahead.

This was the morning that Luke Sullivan, Market Media's new art director, was due to start work with the company.

With three national advertising awards to his credit, a year spent working in New York at one of the top studios, and a reputation as a creative genius, Luke Sullivan had surprised everyone at Market Media when he'd accepted the appointment as head of what must be, for him, a very small design studio.

Comments about his talent aside, the descriptions 'total egotist' and 'slave driver' were some of the nicer things

Andrea had heard said about him since his appointment was announced.

'Luke Sullivan is coming here? As your new boss? Oh, you poor thing!' Stephanie in reception had said to Andrea at the time of the announcement. 'I once had a job temping at an agency where he was art director and you should have heard the studio staff go on about him! They were lucky to get home before nine o'clock some nights! Mind you, it was only the men who complained — he had the women eating out of his hand.'

'Oh, Luke Sullivan never has a problem with women,' agreed Martin, the photographer. 'He gets everything done by using his charm and if that doesn't work, he bulldozes his ideas through anyway. Mind you, he knows his stuff. I worked with Luke a couple of years ago on some photo shoots and he was really good. He knew exactly the effect he wanted and he didn't give the OK until he was satisfied.'

Andrea had listened to all this with

mixed feelings. How would she cope with such a tyrant? It was only a few months since she'd been promoted to her new post as assistant art director to Clive Watson, the gentle, fatherly man whom Luke Sullivan was replacing.

★   ★   ★

Clive was the person who'd helped her most when she'd started in the studio, five years earlier, as a junior artist straight from college. She'd loved working with him, and when he'd recommended her for promotion she'd hugged him in gratitude.

'You deserve it, my girl,' he'd said gruffly. 'I reckon we make a good team, and besides — now I can sit back a bit and let you do all the work!'

Andrea had revelled in the new responsibility but her happiness hadn't lasted.

A few weeks ago, Clive had complained of pains in his chest, and the next morning his wife had phoned to

4

say he'd had a heart attack and was in hospital.

A fortnight later, he was home again; but his doctor had insisted that he retire, and he'd only returned to the studio to pack up his things and say goodbye.

Andrea had watched anxiously as he glanced at the work schedule on the wall. Everything was up to date, although it had taken a few late nights working alone to keep to the advertisers' deadlines. But Clive had nodded his approval, then had stood for a long time studying the pet food campaign that Andrea had started working on while he was in hospital.

'You're doing fine,' he'd said. 'I like that slogan — '*All he needs is love and Chunks*' — I can see you'll cope on your own until the new man arrives.'

With a lump in her throat, Andrea had watched as he moved cautiously between the drawing tables, collecting his pens and inks and unpinning his favourite photos from above his desk.

It was hard to see him being so slow and tired, and so careful with himself.

Suddenly she'd registered the meaning of his words.

'New man? Have they found someone to replace you already?' she'd asked in surprise. Somehow she'd not expected this. She'd felt she'd handled the studio work pretty well, and had imagined that the directors would ask her just to carry on running everything herself.

'Aye, lass, they've someone lined up. And don't think I didn't suggest you for the job. I did, but the directors want someone with more experience. They went after Luke Sullivan and they must have made him a pretty tidy offer because he's starting here the first of next month.'

Andrea knew art directors were fickle people, often moving from one advertising agency to another to work on a more glamorous project, but she couldn't imagine a star from London wanting to work in Lymchester.

'But why would he want to come

here? We're not exactly big time!' she'd protested. 'We haven't any really huge accounts — unless you count Chunks and they only have a few products.'

'I'm not sure, but I've a feeling there's something big in the pipeline. The directors were very cagey when I asked them. But you know, I just can't be bothered, lass. Suddenly I'm really looking forward to doing whatever I feel like doing, without any deadlines to worry about. For starters, Betty and I are thinking of taking a nice holiday in the West Country and I reckon I'll take my sketch book along and take the chance to draw whatever I fancy.'

⋆ ⋆ ⋆

That had been over a month ago. Since then, Andrea had carried on handling all the studio work, doing rough ideas for the Spring Sale advertisements for Folsome Fashions, organising models and photographs for the finished artwork, and making sure that Jeannie, the junior artist, was kept busy.

She'd felt in control and, so far, everything had gone like clockwork. In fact, the more she thought about it, the more annoyed she got that she hadn't been considered for the job on a permanent basis. She might be only twenty-three, but she'd been trained by the best — Clive.

Oh, well, she thought, maybe this Luke will decide we're too small for him and leave after a couple of months.

Deciding that she'd better dress to impress this unknown man who was about to become her boss, she discarded her usual workaday clothes of jeans and sweatshirt and rifled through her wardrobe to find something a bit smarter. She selected a bright tartan pleated skirt and a green silk shirt, which she'd last worn to her sister's wedding.

May as well do it properly, she thought, pulling on sheer black tights and slipping her feet into her high-heeled black pumps. Brushing her dark bob into shape, she looked at her reflection with approval. Yes, green was definitely her colour — she just wished she was a bit taller. If only her nose had been longer and straighter and her mouth not so wide, maybe she'd look more like the high-powered executive sort of art assistant that Luke Sullivan was probably used to.

'Oh, well,' she said out loud, locking the door behind her, 'at least Grant likes me the way I am. More or less.'

The little green sports car, with Grant Carter at the wheel, was by now waiting on the corner.

Usually Grant just leaned over and opened the side door for her. But this morning he jumped out, whistling in appreciation as he looked her up and down with undisguised admiration.

'Hey, what's the occasion? Are we partying tonight?' he asked her, laughing. 'You're looking particularly beautiful!'

'Thank you, kind sir! I'd dress like this every day if I thought I'd get this sort of reaction!'

He grinned at her as he got back behind the wheel of the car and steered it out into the traffic. 'That would suit me!'

As he drove, Andrea turned and gazed at his profile. Good looking, wealthy, ambitious — Grant was the man of her dreams. His thick blond hair was brushed back from a classically handsome face that might have been too perfect if it weren't for his slightly crooked grin, which lit up his face and made him look like a naughty little boy.

Andrea had, by now, been going out with him for a couple of months, and she wondered why he'd ever noticed her when he could have had the pick of all the stylish, elegant girls that he met every day at his work at Mattler Horne.

The only time she'd called for Grant at this national advertising agency — which occupied three floors of glass and pale brick in the centre of town — she'd thought she'd walked into a modelling agency by mistake.

Now, as he headed down town,

weaving his way through the traffic, muttering impatiently when something held him up, Andrea snuggled down into her low-slung leather seat, trying not to flinch at the speed at which he drove and biting her lip when he took corners with the tyres squealing. She'd long since given up asking him to slow down. Grant just couldn't understand anyone being nervous about travelling at high speed and she was determined to get used to it, telling herself that he'd never yet had an accident.

'So, why are you all dressed up then?' he asked. 'A great improvement on your usual gear, I have to say.'

Andrea flushed. Grant couldn't resist an opportunity to tell her that he didn't approve of her normally casual style for the studio. Although she preferred to feel comfortable while working, jeans and a T-shirt were not his idea of smart dressing.

'Our new art director starts this morning,' she reminded him. 'I thought I'd better make a good impression

— but just for today, mind! It won't do to spoil him.'

'Andy, you look so good when you take the trouble — why not do it every day? For me?'

'Oh, Grant,' she sighed, 'don't start that! You know my work in the studio is messy with all that paint and ink. I can't relax when I'm all dressed up. Anyway, don't I always make an effort when we go out together?'

'Sweetie, that's just my point. You have to make an *effort*. But if you spent some time every morning trying to look your best, it would become second nature, wouldn't it? You should look like you do now every day! And believe me, darling, in our line of business it really counts if a girl looks her best at all times.'

'But we're not in the same line of business,' she protested. 'You're an account executive and you have absolutely nothing to do with design and layout. You sit in your smart office, all leather and glass, talking about profit and loss and persuading your clients to spend their money on the good ideas that your art department dreams up for you!'

'I'm not going to start that argument again. If it wasn't for the account executives, then you artistic types wouldn't have a job in the first place. End of story!'

He drew to a halt outside her office and leaned across to open her door.

'Seriously though,' he said, 'when are you going to leave Market Media and come to work at Mattler Home? You know you'd love it and so would I. I'd have you where I could look at you whenever I felt like it!'

He put his arms around her and drew her close. Andrea felt her body melt towards his as she nestled against him.

'I couldn't,' she whispered into his chest. 'Mattler Home is so big, I'd probably be just another junior artist there. I'd never get to be assistant to the art director if I stayed a hundred years!'

'Don't get too set on this career idea of yours,' he warned. 'It's just a job. One of these days you'll be doing something else.'

'Oh, yes? Like your washing and ironing, I suppose?' she joked, climbing out of the cramped little car with as much dignity as possible.

Grant chuckled. 'See you tonight, my love; I'll be round at your flat about nine. We'll do something nice — maybe go to the Colonnade Room.'

He roared off through the traffic towards his office and she turned to hurry across the road, but she stumbled over some rough paving and narrowly missed being run down by a huge camper van.

'Whoops, that was close!' she muttered to herself, catching the driver's eye as he swerved and hooted.

He skidded to a stop, then reversed rapidly.

She stood transfixed in the middle of the road, smiling uncertainly as he wound down the window. She had an impression of thick dark hair and powerful tanned arms. Two quizzical grey eyes looked coolly down at her.

'That piece of advice that your mother might have given you — about looking right and left before you cross the road? — obviously made no lasting impression on you.'

'What?' Andrea couldn't believe her ears. 'How about an apology for the way you were driving? You were coming down the road much too fast!'

'On the contrary, I was looking for a parking space and driving very slowly. You, on the other hand, were sauntering across the road with your mind a million miles away. It's your job as a pedestrian to look out for traffic. If you'd like to live to enjoy another ride in that sardine can you just climbed out of you should try to remember that. And may I just point out that those shoes might be all right for being chauffeured around town but they are definitely not meant for walking.'

He wound up the window and drove off.

Andrea was speechless with rage as she watched the battered camper van disappear around the corner. She couldn't believe her ears. She'd been expecting an apology, not a tirade of abuse from this total stranger. Who did he think he was? What gave him the right to lecture her on how to cross the road and what shoes to wear?

Fuming, she walked on across the road to her office building and pressed the lift button for the fourth floor.

* * *

When Andrea walked into the studio, Jeannie was already there, printing out some layout suggestions for the Covington's Carpets advertisements.

'Hi,' Andrea greeted her. 'Is he in yet?'

Jeannie, who'd started in the art department six months previously as junior layout artist and general dog's-body, knew exactly who she meant.

'Not as far as I know. He's probably

16

in with Tweedledum and Tweedledee. Let's hope he stays there all morning,' she answered.

Tweedledum and Tweedledee were the staff's irreverent nicknames for the directors, Arthur and Cedric Tweed. The names suited them perfectly as one never made a decision without consulting the other, and while one brother talked, the other would nod amiably in agreement. But they didn't interfere with what went on in the studio and never criticised what Andrea produced, usually complimenting her and thanking her politely when she gave them layouts to show to the clients.

'You won't believe what just happened to me!' Andrea continued indignantly. 'A man in a filthy old camper van nearly ran me down, and then gave me a telling-off for wearing such high heels.'

'What a nerve!' said Jeannie, laughing. 'That's a great outfit, by the way. I hope Luke Sullivan will be suitably impressed!'

'Oh, it's not for him.' Andrea flushed.

'I just felt full of the joys of spring, that's all. And it's Tuesday so I'm going to visit Barbara Harris after work.'

'How is she?'

'She seems fine,' said Andrea thoughtfully. 'Every time I go there I offer to read to her but she has all those taped books for when she's on her own. She just likes a good chat, really. I think she gets lonely sometimes.'

Suddenly she was irritated with herself for dressing in anything but her usual clothes just because she was meeting the new art director. He must take me as I am, she thought crossly, kicking off her shoes and slipping her feet into her comfortable flatties.

She went over to her drawing-table, opened a file labelled 'Healthy Grains Incorporated', and found some scribbled notes inside from Tweedledum.

Smiling, she deciphered his familiar shorthand. Healthy Grains Incorporated made an assortment of oat-based snack bars, biscuits and muesli. They wanted a series of four advertisements — with a snappy slogan — for the local newspaper, showing people of various age groups. She switched on her computer, then reached for the phone and pushed a button on the intercom.

'Martin? Hi!'

'Ah — how's my favourite artist? Met your new boss yet?'

'No — but any minute now I expect we'll smell the fire and brimstone and hear his thunderous footfalls in the corridor!' she said, laughing. 'Meanwhile, we've got four adverts for Healthy Grains Incorporated coming up soon and they want a whole family involved. I think we'd better do it photographically — can you organise the models? By Friday?'

'Sure,' said Martin. 'What sort of family are you thinking of?'

'Let's say a couple of small children, a nice Mum and Dad, a teenage boy, and a suitable pair of grandparents — sort of grey-haired but still sparky!'

'OK, will do. And don't worry about Luke Sullivan. He's probably mellowed a lot since the old days — I'm sure you two will get on fine.'

'I hope so.'

She settled down to rough out some ideas, thinking of possible captions for the Healthy Grains adverts and gradually losing herself in her work. The studio was silent as she bent her head over her desk and sketched two toddlers, one of them smiling at a Big Munch cereal bar.

'How about this for a slogan? '*Mum always gives me a Big Munch for lunch!*'' she asked out loud.

'Great!' enthused Jeannie.

'Not bad, but a bit trite,' said a voice from the doorway.

Andrea's head jerked up. She'd heard that voice before, and she'd seen those grey eyes less than an hour ago.

It was the driver of the camper van that had almost run her over, his lanky frame relaxed against the door frame.

He's followed me here — he's completely mad, she thought. How dare he!

'Isn't this a bit excessive?' she asked him coldly. 'Wasn't one lecture enough for today? Or do you make a habit of chasing after every girl in high heels that you see? I think you'd better leave — right now!'

His mouth twitched but he stayed where he was, watching her with undisguised amusement.

'Just leave!' she repeated. 'I'll call security if you don't get going.'

Suddenly Cedric Tweed came fussing into the studio, beaming. He clapped his podgy hand on the man's shoulder.

'Ah, Andrea, I'd like you to meet Luke Sullivan, our new art director.'

* * *

There was a long silence in the studio, broken only by a small stifled gasp from Jeannie.

'Luke, this is Andrea Ross,' Cedric Tweed went on, 'our very able young chief artist. She's been running things in the studio very well for the past few months and I'm sure you'll find her invaluable.'

Andrea felt herself turning scarlet and wished the floor would open up and swallow her.

His eyes never leaving hers, Luke Sullivan reached out and ceremoniously shook her hand.

'I believe Miss Ross and I are already acquainted,' he said, smiling politely as if they'd previously been introduced at some social occasion, but his eyes twinkled wickedly as he watched her embarrassment.

'And Jeannie Parker, our junior; she's been here for six months and she's coming along nicely,' continued Cedric, oblivious to the undercurrent in the room. 'Yes, this is your little team. I'm sure you'll all get on wonderfully well together.'

'Oh, I'm sure we will!' Luke Sullivan agreed, moving across to Jeannie's desk to look at what she was working on.

'Covington's Carpets, I see. And who did these layouts?'

'Andrea — er — Miss Ross did.' The young girl looked up anxiously.

'Mm-mm. Well, I like your presentation, Jeannie.'

So he likes Jeannie's presentation — what about my layouts, thought Andrea, furious.

'Well, I'll leave you all to get to know each other,' said Tweedledee. 'Andrea, perhaps you could put Luke in the picture as to what's on the go at the moment? Luke — I'll see you again at lunchtime in my office.'

He shuffled out of the studio, leaving Andrea staring at the floor, conscious of Luke's eyes on her scarlet face.

She took a deep breath and swallowed hard. Without meeting his eyes, she spoke as calmly as she could.

'Well, Mr Sullivan, as you will see from the work schedule over here, we're working on several campaigns at the moment.'

She led him over to a pin-board attached to the back wall of the studio.

'First of all, Covington's Carpets

want us to do four half-page advertisements for the local papers; they're due to be ready by the end of this month. Then we've just finished these layouts for a dog food manufacturer — Mr Tweed is taking them to the client for approval this afternoon.

'We're also working on this little series of single column adverts for Flower Power — that's a new florist just opened in the shopping centre down the road. And then there's . . . ' Her voice trailed off. He hardly seemed to be listening to her, his eyes scanning the chart and taking in everything faster than she could explain.

'Yep,' he said crisply, 'everything seems to be under control. I'd like to see copies of all the artwork that you've completed in the past three months. And I'd like a list of every client that we've done work for in the past twelve months, no matter how small. Perhaps Jeannie can get all that information for me when she's finished with the Covington's Carpets job?'

He glanced at Jeannie who nodded eagerly.

'And Miss Ross? Or should I say Andrea? We seem to have got off to a bumpy start. Let's try again, first names this time. How about I say, 'Pleased to meet you, Andrea,' and you say, 'Likewise, I'm sure, Luke,' and we take it from there, OK?'

His chiselled features crinkled into a disarming smile and he stretched out his hand. Unable to help herself, she took it and felt the warm, powerful strength in his rough grasp.

Oh, he's wonderful! she found herself thinking involuntarily, and then she told herself sternly that, of course, looking into the mirror each morning he probably knew that.

Flushing, she snatched back her hand. First names would be fine, she decided, but that was it. Nothing more. Another minute of that confident smile and he'd be persuading her to make him a nice cup of tea. Or to sharpen his pencils. He was going to have to remember that she wasn't just a junior layout artist — she was the art director's assistant and had been acting art director for several months.

'OK,' she told him, nodding. 'We'll start again.'

'Right then — I'm pleased to meet you, Andrea.'

'Pleased to meet you, Luke.'

'And I'm glad to see you know when to take good advice,' he went on.

'What do you mean?'

He pointed to her flat shoes. 'A great improvement,' he said. 'What I call sensible footwear. Now, could you show me where we keep the studio stores? I've a feeling we might need to order some materials.'

Seething, and wishing she hadn't kicked off her high heels so quickly, Andrea led him to the store cupboard and angrily snatched open the door.

Too late, she remembered about the mess inside. She'd been meaning to clean out the cupboard before his arrival, but there had never been time.

Trust this man to find her weak spot immediately, she thought, pointing silently to the haphazard heaps of coloured inks, soft pencils and computer discs and cartridges.

'Mmm. Right,' he said dryly, peering in at the disordered shelves. 'Apparently someone around here doesn't have much time for housekeeping.'

'We *have* been very busy,' she told him defensively.

'Well, one messy cupboard doesn't matter too much. We're going to be making some serious changes in this studio in the next couple of weeks anyway.'

Andrea stared at him. 'What do you mean, 'serious changes'?'

'First, we'll be rearranging the studio to facilitate better work flow. Then we'll be getting more up-to-date computers, with new design programmes, which will make you both a lot more useful. But right now I have to go and break bread with our esteemed employer, Mr Tweed. After that I have some shopping to do. See you tomorrow, girls — oh, and you'd better both come into work wearing old clothes. Your spring cleaning could get messy before it's finished.'

Jeannie was the first to break the silence after he left.

'Whoo-hoo!' she breathed. 'Isn't he fabulous?'

''Useful'? Did he say we'd be more useful?' demanded Andrea furiously. 'Just who does he think he is? If he expects us to run around and do his bidding, then he's wrong. And just let him dare to ask me to make him one single cup of tea!'

'Oh, go on, Andy, it was only a joke,' said Jeannie.

'Just because he's worked in the biggest and fanciest art studios doesn't give him the right to sneer at us. Anyway, perhaps Tweedledee won't go along with Mr High-and-Mighty's plans for the studio,' she said slowly. 'He probably won't want to spend money on loads of new stuff.'

But somehow she knew that Luke would get his way.

Tweedledee would be delighted to be thought of as a forward-looking captain of industry, and by half-way through lunch he'd have agreed to anything his marvellous new art director wanted.

In no time at all, everyone would be doing things exactly as the charming and persuasive Luke Sullivan wanted them done, and there was absolutely nothing she could do to stop it.

Lunch with the Boss

As soon as the studio clock showed five-thirty, Andrea packed away her work. She was usually the last to leave, and when she asked Jeannie to lock up for once, she sensed the young girl's unspoken surprise.

'Meeting Grant tonight?' asked the younger girl in a neutral tone. It was no secret that Jeannie didn't like Andrea's boyfriend.

'I just don't know what you see in him,' was all she'd say whenever Andrea pressed her for a reason for her antipathy.

She's just jealous, thought Andrea. Privately she felt sorry for Jeannie, who lived with her invalid father and seemed to have almost no life of her own outside work.

'Yes, I am seeing Grant later,' she said now, 'but first I've promised to look in on Barbara.'

Once out of the building, Andrea hurried across town towards Tower Mansions. She knew Barbara looked forward to her visits and hated her to be even five minutes late.

She spent a few moments choosing a bunch of sweet-smelling stocks from the flower-seller on the corner, and then took the stairs two at a time up to the blind girl's flat.

Andrea had met Barbara Harris through Helpline, a group of volunteers who gave a few hours each week to take disabled people shopping, help with their housework, write their letters, or do whatever else they needed.

Barbara, blinded in a motor accident the year before, was fiercely independent, and managed her own housework, but needed a friend.

Andrea had begun by visiting her every Tuesday to read aloud to her, but soon she found herself popping in two or three times a week after work, just to chat for half an hour or so.

In fact, Barbara had probably become

Andrea's best friend. After all their heart-to-hearts, there was nothing they didn't know about each others' hopes and dreams.

'Hi, Andy!' said Barbara as she opened the door. 'I'd hoped it was you. Are those flowers for me? Mmm . . . scented stocks, they're lovely. Thanks.'

Andrea always marvelled at her friend's sense of smell. She'd read that when someone lost the use of one sense, the other senses improved to make up for it, but Barbara was incredible. She could name every perfume that Andrea wore, recognised fruit before it was even out of the packet, and could even tell if she was carrying a newspaper — just from the smell.

'So, what's new? How was your day? How's the incomparable Grant? Tell me all!' Barbara busied herself in her small kitchen off the lounge, arranging the flowers in a vase.

'My day was just awful, thanks.'

'Come on, Andy, that bad? Oh, of course — today's the day your new art director arrived! Is he the problem?

What's he like?'

'He's the problem, all right,' Andrea answered bleakly. 'He's so bossy and overbearing — and critical of everything. You know what sort of man he is? He nearly ran me over in the street and didn't even apologise. In fact he gave me a lecture — right there in the street — on what sort of shoes I should wear! And then he came into the office, and I thought . . . '

Suddenly the funny side of her day struck her and she started to giggle.

'Oh, Barbs, I thought he was a crazy guy — that he'd come after me to give me another talking to — and I told him that if he didn't get out I'd call the security guard!'

Tears of mirth rolled down her cheeks as she relived the scene.

'And then old Tweedledee came in and introduced him to me as my new boss! What a start!'

She rolled over on the sofa, giggling helplessly, with Barbara joining in.

'Well, it can't be that bad. At least

you're laughing about it now! What does he look like?'

'Well . . . ' Andrea considered. 'He's very good-looking, I suppose, in a boney sort of way. He's tall and stringy with dark hair — and very tanned, as though he's lived outdoors all his life. But he's so arrogant! He thinks he just has to smile and we'll jump through hoops for him. He's definitely not going to be an easy person to work for. I mean, the way he marched in and told us he's going to change everything from the first day — without even giving us a chance to say what we thought.'

'Probably because he knew you'd argue with him,' suggested Barbara reasonably. 'I expect he could feel your hostile vibes a mile off.'

'Oh dear, do you think so? But he's impossible. It's a pity, really; I was all set to try to like him. I even put on a nice outfit today specially to impress him. Never again! I doubt he'd notice if I came to work in my pyjamas, so long as I wore sensible shoes! Anyway,' she added ruefully, 'I'll just have to see how it goes. Jeannie seems to think he's wonderful. Let's change the subject — how about coffee? I'll make it.'

Through in the kitchen, as she laid the tray, she carried on talking to Barbara over her shoulder. Before the accident which changed her life forever, Barbara had been a commercial photographer and she loved to hear about Andrea's latest studio work. Every little detail interested her and she often gave Andrea good ideas for a new slant on an advertisement.

'Something new came in for Healthy Grains Incorporated today — they want a series of adverts showing how healthy their stuff is. I've designed layouts showing every age group enjoying their snack bars and I think it's going to go well. We'll be using Martin for the photographs.'

'Martin's good, isn't he?' said Barbara wistfully. 'I remember he did a beautiful series of food pictures for a calendar once; really good lighting. You felt that you could have picked the apples off the page.'

'Yes, and he's great to work with. He never gets into a flap like some of those madly creative guys. I did a shoot once with Max Wilson and by the time we'd finished, Max was hysterical and the model was in tears! So anyway,' said Andrea, handing her a cup of coffee, 'what's your news?'

'Nothing much. When I was putting out the rubbish I spoke to the woman who's just moved into the flat next door. She sounds nice but she works all day so I don't suppose I'll see much of her.'

'Well, why not invite her round here one evening?'

Andrea worried about her friend who, although she had become self-sufficient and was able to do her own shopping and housework, was terribly shy and found it hard to make friends. She wished she could persuade her to join a club of some sort, but every suggestion she made met with a gentle refusal. Not that Barbara didn't have plenty to occupy her. She 'read' a lot using tapes, loved listening to music, and had recently started making surprisingly good clay models of animals.

'Anyway,' Andrea went on, 'I think it's definitely time you met Grant. You know so much about him, and he knows all about you — I just have to get the two of you together. How about this weekend? Saturday afternoon? Maybe we could all go for a drive?'

'What, in his famous sports car? Where would I sit? On the bonnet? No, I've a better idea: you bring him here and I'll give you a nice tea. It's time I tried my hand at baking again.'

★　★　★

After leaving Barbara's, Andrea rushed home. She was much later than she'd intended to be and Grant would arrive at any minute, expecting to find her all dressed and ready for the Colonnade Room.

The sitting-room was in its usual

mess — last night's coffee cup still on top of the TV and newspapers scattered around. Grant hated disorder and she rushed about, scooping up the papers, plumping up the cushions and brushing toast crumbs off the sofa. She wished she'd been born naturally tidy, as some people seemed to be. As it was, she managed to keep just on top of the rising tide of chaos by having energetic clean-ups whenever she was expecting visitors. Perhaps Grant would just pull up at the door and toot, as he often did, and she could run down to the car.

The phone shrilled just as she was hurriedly stepping out of her skirt and wondering if she had time for a shower.

It was Grant.

'I'm sorry, Pumpkin. I've got to call it off for tonight. We've got clients here from Japan and yours truly has to show them the sights. Take them out to dinner and keep them happy at a few clubs afterwards. The usual stuff.'

'Oh, Grant, no! What a bore for you. Perhaps I could come too?'

She'd been looking forward to telling him about her disastrous day, to burying her head in his shoulder and letting him comfort her.

'Not this time, Andy, sorry. It's not as if these guys have brought their wives with them. You'd be bored by all the business talk.'

She swallowed her disappointment silently.

'OK. Enjoy yourself. I'll see you tomorrow.'

'Not cross with me, are you, Pumpkin? I'll make it up to you at the weekend. We'll think of somewhere nice to go, just the two of us.'

'Well, Barbara's invited us to tea on Saturday and I'd really like the two of you to meet,' she suggested hesitantly. She knew that having tea with one of her friends was probably not Grant's idea of a good time.

'OK, sweetie, anything you say. Maybe I'll see you tomorrow, but I don't think I'll be able to pick you up in the morning — I'll probably be going in later than usual. I'll phone you sometime. Cheerio for now!'

She felt deflated as she put down the phone. Another date cancelled at the last minute. It wasn't Grant's fault — he had to put his work first — but she had to admit, he was often maddeningly off-hand, changing his plans, and hers, at a moment's notice.

Don't go getting possessive, Andrea, she told herself. Grant's got every right to do what he wants. And so have I. There's no commitment from either of us.

But he hadn't even asked her how her day had gone, even though he'd known that she was worried about meeting her new boss.

She was angry with herself, but she couldn't prevent her eyes filling with tears as she wandered into the kitchen to make herself a lonely supper.

⋆   ⋆   ⋆

By lunchtime the next day she was bone weary. When she and Jeannie had arrived at work, Luke had been ready for action with his sleeves rolled up as he greeted them at the door of the studio. Their desks had already been pushed into the centre of the room.

'Dressed for some real work I see — much better!' he said, looking with approval at Andrea's blue jeans and sweatshirt.

'Ooh, Andy, don't you think he's cool?' hissed Jeannie as they hung up their coats. 'He's so good looking and when he smiles — wow!'

'Mmm.' Andrea's mumbled reply was non-committal.

The firm set of his mouth indicated a man who was used to getting his own way — maybe he could fool young Jeannie into thinking he was cool, but he wasn't going to fool her.

Luke pulled out desk and cupboard drawers, and directed operations as Andrea and Jeannie sorted through their contents, throwing out the accumulation of out-of-date art work prepared for campaigns long since forgotten, unused roughs and pages of discarded copy.

'Out it goes,' he said ruthlessly. 'If it's not currently being worked on, put it on the pile.'

Andrea had always known that Clive didn't have much of a filing system for all the art work done over the years, and she'd carried on where he'd left off. So, as the morning wore on, the pile grew steadily higher. Sketches for projects long since forgotten were unearthed and discarded. Luke must have thought he'd come to work in some fusty old backwater.

Well, compared with where he'd been working before, Market Media probably *was* impossibly old-fashioned, Andrea told herself.

They'd never even done a TV campaign or a full-colour advertisement for a national magazine. All then work, so far, had been for local stores and businesses.

With a pang, Andrea saw Luke toss aside one of her first efforts, a drawing that had been used in an advertisement for a children's clothing shop. She remembered how thrilled she'd been to see her first art work printed in the local paper, and she snatched it back.

'Not this one. I'll keep it. I'll take it home.'

He raised his eyebrows.

'Sentimental value,' she admitted coolly. 'This is the first thing I did here, straight from art school.'

'Not bad for a first effort,' he said critically, pushing back his dark hair with a decidedly dusty hand. 'Have we still got the account?'

'No. The shop closed down. Not because of my artwork — they were doing quite well — but because the owner died.'

'Well, if things go according to plan we'll be soon be so busy we won't need all these small accounts,' he answered. 'This studio will soon have so much work that you won't know what's hit you.'

Andrea stared at him.

'Why? Have you brought a big new client to the studio with you?'

'No, this is something Mr Tweed has been working on for a long time and things are about to come to a head any day now. It's his project so I won't spoil his fun. I'll let him tell you once we have the account confirmed. All I can say is that it's big. It's a national account, and once we get it we'll be doing press adverts for every paper in the country, as well as TV spots, full-colour magazine adverts — the works.'

'Fantastic!' said Jeannie, her eyes shining. 'When will we know for sure that the client has signed with us?'

'By next week at the latest. In the meantime, I've set up some fast-track training for both of you so that you can learn to use a new design programme that I've brought over from the States.'

'Training?' queried Andrea. 'Can't we just pick up how it works as we go along? The system we're using now . . .'

'What you're using now is completely outdated. This new programme is state-of-the art and I don't think any other studio is using it yet. We'll have a big advantage over the opposition once you two have got used to it. So, I've arranged coaching for both of you with a specialist,' he said, 'starting tonight straight after work, actually — I hope that's all right. By tomorrow we'll all have new computers with the programme installed and I've no doubt that within a couple of weeks you'll wonder how you ever managed without it.'

Andrea seethed. How high-handed could he get?

'Tonight is not convenient, I'm afraid. I have a date,' she snapped. 'I'll have to start my training tomorrow.'

'Sorry,' said Luke, 'but you start your training this evening. You'll just have to tell him it's off. I take it your date was with the driver of that little tin can that brought you to work yesterday?'

To her annoyance, she flushed.

'That 'little tin can' is a fabulous car,' she defended, 'a lot better than some dirty great tank belching out black smoke.'

'Tch Tch! I can see those wheels are important to you; or is it the driver who is so attractive?'

'Well, the driver's important to me, too,' she admitted coolly. 'He's also in advertising. His name's Grant Carter and he's an account executive at Mattler Horne. You'll probably meet him soon — he often pops in to pick me up after work.'

There was a sudden silence in the studio that made her look up from wiping the shelves. Luke's expression was forbidding and there was a cold, warning glint in his eye.

'This boyfriend of yours will never — ever — come into this studio,' he said slowly. 'Is that clear? And you will never — ever — discuss your work with him.'

'Why on earth not?' she asked, genuinely puzzled. Of course she discussed her work with Grant. She loved what she did and enjoyed telling him about what had happened in the studio during the day.

'This is something you've got to remember,' said Luke icily. 'The art studio in every advertising agency is the heart of the place. This is where it all happens. Any ideas, any new campaigns, start right here. And it is *not* smart to let the competition know what you're doing.'

'But Grant's hardly our competition!' she snapped defensively. 'Mattler Horne are an enormous agency and nothing we do here could possibly interest them. Besides, he deals with the clients and probably never goes into the studio.'

'Account executives are forever coming in to ask about artwork,' returned Luke, 'and even a chance remark about what we're doing here could be used against us if the wrong person heard it.'

Jeannie was listening to all this with wide eyes.

'Do you mean industrial espionage?' she breathed.

'Something like that,' he said. 'So don't talk to anyone about what we're doing in this studio, even if they've nothing to do with the advertising business. They might have a brother or sister who does.'

Andrea listened in disbelief.

'Oh, come on,' she mocked. 'Surely you're over-reacting? We're not dealing in top-secret scientific work here! And anyway, Grant isn't the type who'd ever repeat what he heard.'

'I mean what I say,' he said shortly. 'Nobody is to come into this studio who isn't a member of our own staff.'

Andrea's temper flared. 'I think you're being insulting,' she said. 'None of my friends, or Jeannie's, would act as a spy. And Grant's been coming up here for months and Mr Tweed has never objected.'

'My dear child, neither of the Mr Tweeds are very street-wise and probably haven't even heard of industrial espionage. But a lot of nasty things happen out there. I'm not saying your Grant is a spy — but he does work for a rival agency and from now on he is not to come inside this studio.'

What rubbish, fumed Andrea silently, turning away to fill another plastic bag with old artwork from the drawers. The man's paranoid. I won't even tell Grant; he'd explode if he knew Luke thought he was a potential spy!

'And I trust I can rely on your absolute discretion when you're talking to him outside working hours,' continued Luke. 'You are never to mention anything about your work, to him or to anyone else, is that clearly understood? By both of you?'

Both girls nodded wordlessly.

★   ★   ★

By lunchtime the room looked completely different. As a result of Luke's shopping expedition the day before, new sets of drawers had been delivered to the studio. Pale grey and very modern looking, they were wide enough to take the largest layout pages which were now filed neatly under the name of the client.

Some of the old cupboards had been moved out into the passage, the desks and tables had been rearranged, and suddenly there was masses of space and everything seemed a lot brighter.

'The next step is paint,' said Luke, surveying the results of their work. 'I have a painter coming in tomorrow. What colour walls would you ladies like?'

Andrea said nothing. Let him choose, she thought. It's his studio now and he's going to do exactly what he wants anyway. He won't listen to anything we want.

But Jeannie answered him eagerly.

'Don't you think a very pale blue would look nice? We could get some gloss and do the woodwork too — that would look great.'

He glanced at his watch.

'Right, that sounds good; let's go shopping. But I think the first thing we need is a spot of lunch. Can you recommend a decent place to eat around here?'

'The Trattoria,' said Jeannie promptly. 'It's just around the corner.'

'Thanks, but I'm not hungry,' said Andrea, unwilling to spend her lunch break with this overbearing man.

'Nonsense, you must be starving,' said Luke. 'Get your coats, both of you.'

Andrea found herself picking up her bag in spite of herself.

'What a way to spend a morning,' giggled Jeannie as they fetched their coats. 'I haven't done this much housework for ages!'

'Rather a waste of time,' Andrea replied. 'What about all the studio work that's piling up?'

'What's got into you? I think everything looks lovely now, and there's nothing that can't wait until tomorrow.' The younger girl was delighted. 'And imagine, he's taking us out to lunch! He's turned out to be much nicer than we thought he'd be, hasn't he, Andy?'

'I'm glad you think so,' she said shortly.

★　★　★

Settled comfortably at a corner table of The Trattoria, with a bowl of spaghetti bolognaise and a glass of white wine in front of her, Andrea relaxed and studied Luke, while Jeannie plied him with questions.

With his tall body draped casually across a chair which seemed too small for him, he folded his muscular brown arms across his chest and answered Jeannie's hesitant enquiries about his past.

Their new art director made his work in America and his advertising awards sound like things that had happened a long time ago that were now of no importance to him. In fact, if she hadn't known better, Andrea would have said that he sounded pretty modest about his achievements.

'New York was a great experience, but nobody can live there for too long if they want to stay sane,' he said, casually dismissing his year with the world's largest advertising agency. 'I was lucky to work for great clients who just went along with all the crazy ideas I threw at them. Americans are fun to work with, willing to try anything, the wilder the better. But I had to come back before I went totally nuts. You can't live properly in a place that big.'

'What do you mean, 'live properly'?' asked Andrea. 'I wouldn't have thought there was much you couldn't do in New York.'

He turned to look at her.

'But there are no mountains there,' he said simply. 'Their idea of open space is a park, for goodness' sake. You're surrounded by buildings and people every hour of the day. It's definitely not my kind of place.'

That accounts for the camper van, she realised. Who'd have thought he was a fresh air fiend?

'What made you choose to come to Lymchester?' she asked. 'After New York it must seem pretty tame here.'

'Well, I lived near here as a child, about a thousand years ago. But it was the size and location of this town that really attracted me. From where I'm living it's only ten minutes to the countryside, with great mountain walks in every direction. I can't wait to get my boots on and get out there.'

What a strange mixture this man is, she thought. Instead of the slick, smooth-talking advertising man she'd expected, he was a tousled giant, so careless of his image that he appeared almost unkempt, shunning the bright lights and the crowds.

And interested in only one thing — climbing mountains.

Strange that someone like that should be such a creative, driven genius when it came to advertising.

'And what about you?' He broke into her thoughts. 'What do you do when you're not hard at work?'

'Oh, nothing special,' she answered. 'I go to the gym as often as I can and I try to fit in a good run over the weekends.'

Who are you kidding, Andrea, she asked herself. It's been a month since you set foot inside the gym and when did you last run further than the bus stop?

'Ever been up the mountains around here?'

'I used to climb a lot when I was at college, back home in Scotland, but since I've been living down here, I've just never had the opportunity,' she said, rather regretfully. 'And Grant doesn't — that is, nobody I know likes camping or anything like that.'

His mouth twitched. 'Not the outdoor type, is he? That's a pity.'

'Oh, it doesn't matter. I mean, there's plenty to do. We go to clubs and see films . . . ' She tailed off.

Apart from going out to restaurants or nightclubs in the evenings, there wasn't much else that she and Grant did together, except for going shopping at weekends.

I must change that, she decided, wondering how she was going to persuade Grant to don running shoes and join her jogging round the park.

'And your graphic art?' Luke enquired briskly. 'Where did you train?'

She told him about her art college and about how working for Market Media was her first job since graduating.

'You really seem to enjoy your work — that's good,' he commented. 'And you've got an original turn of mind, which is just about the most important thing for anyone in an art studio.' He looked at her with approval. 'Yep, I think old Mr Tweed was right: we'll make a great team.'

'Once we've learned to be a bit more useful to you?' Andrea's sour rejoinder slipped out before she could stop it.

He looked genuinely puzzled, then gave an amused snort. 'You do take things seriously, don't you? I was only teasing. Mind you,' he continued thoughtfully, 'that's the trouble with women: absolutely no sense of humour and too blooming temperamental — particularly the artistic ones.'

'I am not . . . ' she started angrily, and then caught his eye. He was laughing at her again.

'You're not what? Artistic or temperamental?'

He's impossible, she thought crossly.

'Andrea's very artistic,' chimed in
Jeannie loyally. 'She does really super
stuff.'

'I'm sure she does.' He gave her a
long look. 'Well, just as long as she's not
too bossy, we should get along fine.
One thing I can't stand is a bossy
woman!'

'Bossy?' she choked. 'Me — bossy?
You of all people have got a nerve to say
that to me. Bossy is the last thing I am.'

'Good,' he said calmly. 'One bossy
person in the studio is about all there's
room for. And that person is going to
be me.'

'I don't doubt that for a minute.' She
lifted her chin. 'I've seen you in action
already, remember?'

'I was trying to be a true gentleman
and not refer to it, but since you insist
on bringing up your lack of road
sense . . .'

She choked. '*My* lack of road sense!

You were going too fast and you know it! If there'd been a policeman around I could have reported you.'

'On the contrary, you were falling all over the road like a drunken sailor. When I saw you I thought to myself, now there goes a girl who can't hold her liquor.'

Jeannie exploded with mirth and Andrea realised once again that he was pulling her leg.

'What about that paint we're supposed to be buying?' she asked coldly. 'Or are we going to have two-hour lunch breaks from now on?'

He stood up suddenly.

'Nope. This was a special occasion lunch. After today, you'll get a ten-minute lunch break to finish your bread and water and then it's back to the treadmill.'

It didn't make it any better that Jeannie giggled appreciatively.

⋆ ⋆ ⋆

Grant had phoned the studio while they were out and had left a message for Andrea. He couldn't make it again that evening; the Japanese clients were still in town.

Just as well, she thought. I've got to get through this afternoon first, and then I've got to face this stupid computer lesson.

Anticipating a miserable time, she set off for the college straight from work that evening, with Jeannie bubbling happily at her side.

However, much to her surprise, Andrea found the new programme easier to operate than she'd thought. It had taken her a long time to learn their old programme and she'd always felt she wasn't particularly good with the technical stuff.

'The thing about this new software is that it's very user-friendly,' enthused their tutor, a young man who looked as though he'd been born sitting in front of a computer screen, so quickly did his fingers fly around the keyboard. 'And you'll find it very easy to switch to this from your old system.'

By the end of the evening, she and Jeannie had grasped the basics of the programme, and Andrea could see that it was faster and a lot more useful than the one they'd been used to.

'Jeannie, this is going to be a great improvement. I suppose I owe that horrible man some sort of an apology. Not that he's going to get one after the way he carried on at lunch.'

Exciting News!

Walking into the studio the following morning, the first thing that caught her eye was a huge old wartime poster pinned to the notice board. It showed an evil little man with his head pressed to a wall while two women chattered gaily on the other side of it.

'*REMEMBER WALLS HAVE EARS*', warned the caption.

Luke noticed her reading it.

'Just a reminder,' he said laconically.

'My lips are sealed,' she replied pertly. 'Now, of course, all we need are a few secrets to practise our silence on!'

'Patience, woman. Patience.'

Andrea noticed that, since yesterday afternoon, he had decorated the walls of his office with big black and white photographs of mountains.

She studied them, enthralled in spite of herself.

'These are marvellous pictures,' she exclaimed. 'Where were they taken?'

'The ones on that wall I took in Morocco, and these over here, the Rockies.'

'So you did escape from New York sometimes. Did you take all of these pictures?'

'All of them except this one.'

She studied the photograph of an ant-like figure clinging on upside down to a rock which itself appeared to be hanging out into space.

'This is you!' she exclaimed when she realised. 'Do you really do this sort of climbing? I'd be terrified!'

'Don't let the angle of the picture fool you — it wasn't really as difficult as it looks. But I must admit I've given up that sort of cliff-hanging. I get my kicks from ordinary upright climbing these days.'

'What happened, did old age finally catch up with you?' she joked.

'Something like that.' His voice was remote. 'Actually, I witnessed a very bad accident and decided it was time to scale down a bit.'

She waited for him to go on, and when he didn't, she glanced at him. His face was rigid and he was staring blindly at the photograph.

Maybe it was the friend who'd taken the photo who'd had the accident, she thought in dismay.

Tactfully, she turned away and went to hang up her coat.

However, as she passed his desk she noticed a photograph pushed half-way under his computer and pulled it towards her, looking with open curiosity at the vivacious face of a laughing girl. A tumble of blonde curls caressed the girl's shoulders and '*All my love, Hailey*' was scrawled boldly across the corner in green ink. Probably his girlfriend — and a model by the look of her.

Andrea cleared her throat and said brightly, 'And this picture? Did you take this one, too?'

He turned round.

'What? Where did you find that?'

He almost snatched the photo from her, shoving it into the top drawer of his desk without looking at it. He slammed the drawer and turned away. There was obviously to be no further discussion on that subject.

Andrea told herself that she wasn't all that interested anyway, but she couldn't help wondering whether the beautiful Hailey had accompanied him to England or if she'd been left behind in the States.

Their new computers had been delivered to the studio and Luke spent some time unpacking them and fiddling about with wires and plugs. Then he expertly installed the new programme.

'Now, these things are not going to bite you,' he announced as he assembled the keyboards and wired the monitors to a printer. 'Right, let's see how much you two ladies learned last night.'

Andrea sat down in front of her screen and her mind promptly went blank.

'Um — where's the 'On' switch for

this thing?' she asked in a small voice, irked to see that Jeannie already seemed to know just what to do.

'Give yourself two weeks and you'll be an expert,' said Luke, reaching over her shoulder and tapping out the commands to bring the new graphics programme on to the screen. Andrea felt herself completely engulfed in his arms as he leaned over her, and in confusion she looked down at his hands on the keyboard. Big, masculine hands, with blunt fingers which looked as if they'd be more at home chopping wood than tapping at computer keys.

'There you are, carry on from there,' he said finally. 'Just practise working on it this morning and if you have any questions, ask me.'

He went into his office and she and Jeannie were left to play around with the new software.

Andrea typed in the words 'BOSSY BOOTS'. Remembering her lesson of the night before, she made the letters stretch across the screen and then swell out in the middle. She added little puffs of smoke and flashes of lightning, then drew wavy lines above and below. A frame of flowers completed the picture and she was just starting to add some stars to this creation when she realised that Luke was standing behind her.

'Getting the hang of it, I see,' he said in amusement.

'Sort of,' she said guiltily as she hurriedly pressed the 'delete' button, then watched her cartoon fade as she felt his eyes burning into the back of her neck.

'I'm going out for lunch,' she said hastily. 'Coming, Jeannie?'

*   *   *

That night, Grant phoned to suggest a meal at a steakhouse. 'I haven't eaten anything halfway decent for two days,' he grumbled. 'Nothing but meeting after meeting, with nasty little snacks instead of proper food.'

'Oh, poor Grant,' sympathised Andrea.

'Why don't you come round here to my flat? I could easily make us a nice pasta dish.'

'No, thanks. Let's go out properly. When you mess about in that oversized cupboard you call a kitchen it just makes me nervous. No, you go and get dressed in something gorgeous, and listen out for my car in about an hour.'

Andrea was tired. Although she'd enjoyed exploring the capabilities of the new computer software, she had been concentrating on the screen all day and could feel the beginning of a headache behind her eyes. The last thing she felt like was getting dressed up and having a late night.

But she hadn't seen Grant for two whole days so there was nothing for it but to have a hot shower and an aspirin and hope she'd feel better by eight o'clock.

As she was stepping out of the shower, the phone rang.

'Miss Ross? Hello, my dear, this is Peter McVitty.'

'Oh, Mr McVitty, how nice to hear from you,' she said with real pleasure.

Peter McVitty ran the local branch of Helpline, and when Andrea had volunteered to work for the organisation a year ago, it was he who had put her in touch with Barbara. Every few months he phoned to see how they were both getting on.

'Everything fine with Mrs Harris?' he enquired now.

'Oh yes, I think so,' she replied, towelling dry her hair while she talked. 'She's much more cheerful these days, although she's still quite lonely. I wish she'd get out and meet more people. But compared with when I first met her, she hardly seems like the same person.'

'I'm sure a lot of that is due to your concern and companionship, my dear. She's lucky to have found such a friend in you.'

'It works both ways,' Andrea assured him. 'I really like Barbara and she's good company. It's not me who's doing her favour by visiting her — in fact, it's often a case of her cheering *me* up!'

'That's fine then, Miss Ross. But any problems, just call me.'

Andrea said goodbye and hung up, thinking that signing up as a volunteer worker for Helpline was one of the best things she'd ever done. Barbs was a real friend now.

She snatched her yellow silk dress from its hanger in the wardrobe and slipped it over her head. Oh dear, it needed pressing and there was Grant, tooting his car horn down in the street already.

She balanced on one leg, wriggled her foot into high heels and pulled a brush through her still-damp hair. Running to the window she waved out at him. Grant hated to be kept waiting.

*   *   *

On Thursday morning, both Tweedledum and Tweedledee came into the studio, smiling broadly.

'Ladies, we have some very good news,' announced Tweedledum, while his brother stood nodding approvingly behind him. 'As of yesterday, the United Northern Insurance Company have given their national account to Market Media.'

'Oh, Mr Tweed, that's fantastic!' exclaimed Andrea. 'They're an enormous company. They must be one of the biggest insurers in the country!'

'Certainly amongst the top five, definitely, yes,' agreed Tweedledum, his round face suffused with pleasure. 'I can tell you now that my brother and I have been after this extremely big fish for some months and it was a combination of good luck and our good name that won us this account. They've been unhappy with their present agency for some time, and once they heard that we had Luke Sullivan as our new art director — well, that decided them. United Northern's account is going to make a big difference to us all.'

'Well, congratulations, Mr Tweed and

— er — Mr Tweed,' said Andrea. 'This is really going to put us on the map. Will we be handling all their advertising? TV adverts, too?'

'Everything, my dear Miss Ross, everything. TV, radio spots, the daily press, monthlies, billboards, the lot. Something new for you, I know. You and young Jeannie will be very busy from now on.'

The brothers Tweed bustled out and left Andrea and Jeannie staring at Luke.

'OK, you heard what the man said.' His tone was businesslike. 'Jeannie, from now on I'm putting you in charge of all the local jobs that come in from our regular clients. This means that you'll be given a lot more responsibility. Think you can handle it? Good. You can start by finishing off those layouts for Healthy Grains Incorporated that Andrea was busy with the other day. Any problems, ask me.'

Jeannie glowed, thrilled to bits.

Luke turned to Andrea. 'Right, let's get down to work.'

She pulled up a stool and sat opposite him at his work table.

'Now,' he said. 'I have to make one thing clear. As the art director, I'm responsible for everything that leaves this studio. I know you've been used to working on your own, but from now on you're going to have to get my approval before you do anything. Is that understood?'

'Yes,' she said shortly.

'Is that a sulk I see? Doesn't suit you one bit,' he said easily. 'If you had ever worked anywhere else but here, you'd know this is standard practice in all studios. No artist is allowed to send out work to the clients without the director's approval. But,' he added, softening, 'I'm aware that you've been the brains behind some of the better advertising that's been done here in the past year, so are you ready for some real work? I'm warning you, you're in for a rough ride from now on, so if you don't want the responsibility and long hours that I expect from an assistant art director, then now is the time to say so and I'll hire someone else.'

'You will not!' Andrea exploded indignantly. 'I've never missed a deadline in my life.'

'All right. It's just that I've worked with girls your age before and most of them want to rush off at five o'clock. But that's not how I do things. When there's something to be finished, we'll finish it. Never mind the boyfriends waiting on the pavement.'

How dare he talk to me like this, she thought furiously. How else did his lordship think we got the work out on time before he got here?

She bit her lip and forced herself to keep listening.

'Now, what United Northern want first of all is a new TV spot, tying in with a national press advertising campaign. We're looking at half-page adverts in the Sunday supplements, the financial weeklies, and about ten of the more suitable women's magazines. United Northern have checked the breakdown of their client profile and discovered that there are far more women than they thought who make the decisions on family insurance policies.'

In spite of herself, Andrea was fascinated. Her thoughts raced as she realised this would be the most exciting job she'd ever worked on.

'What do we tackle first?' she queried.

'We've got to decide on a theme that will give instant product recognition no matter where people see it. Luckily they're an old company and have been around for a long time. So that's easier in some ways than trying to introduce the public to something completely new.'

'But it also means they're probably quite set in their ways and have very definite ideas of what they want,' she added, thinking of all the insurance adverts she'd seen.

'Well, we might persuade them to go for something a little bit different but they won't be too keen on something completely over the top.'

'Pity!' said Andrea flippantly. 'We could have a rap group singing their praises. That would be something a bit different.'

'Not a bad idea, but we'll have to keep that for something with a younger market,' said Luke. 'But you've got the idea — something that will make people sit up and take notice. The profile of a United Northern client shows their average age to be thirty-nine years old, so rap isn't going to appeal to them. Sixty-seven per cent of them are female, and the spread of clients is countrywide, with more of them in the North than the South. Of course, they started in Scotland in 1924 but since then they've opened branches all over.'

'Client profile,' wondered Andrea. 'I've never even heard of that.'

'All the bigger companies get a picture of their average customer by running their details through their computers,' explained Luke patiently. 'Terribly useful things, computers! Before they did this, they were often using advertising that simply didn't appeal to most of the people who bought their products.'

'I suppose we've just never had clients big enough to bother with that sort of thing.'

'Well, that's all changed now,' said Luke with a grin. 'Welcome to the big time, Andy!'

He's not at all bad, she thought unwillingly.

'What about the copywriting?' she asked. 'We used to have a copywriter but he left last year, and after that Clive and I just wrote the captions and the copy ourselves and we seemed to manage fine.'

'I write my own copy, always have,' he said briefly. 'It's far easier to do the visuals and the copy together; you get a complete picture that way.'

'And the TV spots?' she asked. 'We don't actually film those ourselves do we?

'No, we leave the technicalities to a

video production company, but we're still very involved in the making of it. We choose the characters, give the film people the script we want, and sit in on all the filming. You'll probably enjoy that part of it and you'll learn a lot.'

He really means to let me be part of the whole thing, thought Andrea in amazement. Suddenly he seemed to be opening more doors for her than she'd ever thought possible.

There's probably a catch, she cautioned herself. He'll just take me along to all these things so that he can boss me around in public. Well, if he tries to do that, then he'll discover that I'm not so easy to push around.

Meeting Grant's Mother

Andrea pulled out her sketch pad and started doodling, her mind sifting through possibilities. Luke handed her a thick sheaf of papers.

'Here are copies of all the advertising done by United Northern for the past year. You can get some idea of what they've been doing up until now,' he said, bending over her to flick through them.

She felt the sheer animal magnetism of the man and heard her treacherous heart beginning to pound. She drew away from him quickly and was aware of his amused smile.

'I still can't understand why they should choose us,' she muttered, hoping he wasn't able to read her thoughts. 'If companies are tired of their old agencies, don't they usually invite a lot of others to put forward their ideas for a campaign and then choose the best?'

'That's what they usually do,' agreed Luke. 'But in this case a little family connection worked wonders. The chairman of United Northern is the older brother of Cedric Tweed's wife. That helped. In fact, there are some pretty disappointed art directors right now who can't understand why all their beautiful campaigns didn't get a look in!'

'So when Mr Tweed said they'd been working on it for months, he probably meant he'd been wining and dining his brother-in-law at vast expense!' She snorted. 'Is that how big business works?'

'Sometimes.'

She started flicking through the pile of glossy reference books that Luke had brought with him to the office, most of them from America. Advertisements from all over the world for every kind of business. She was entranced, and before she knew it, it was time to stop for the day.

To her dismay, Andrea realised she'd

drawn absolutely nothing. She started to apologise but Luke cut her short.

'Hey, I sometimes sit for days without inspiration striking. Don't worry. We'll work on it tomorrow. Let's call it a day.'

They went down in the lift together, and Andrea was conscious of his solid height looming comfortingly next to her, her head barely reaching his shoulder.

Everything about him seemed larger and rougher than she was used to. Grant's slight frame was always elegantly dressed, his hair styled and his shoes shining.

She stole a look at Luke's rather elderly leather moccasins and well-worn jeans. She tried to imagine him in a suit and couldn't. How did this man ever get to work in a New York advertising agency looking the way he did?

'Is the sardine can waiting or can I give you a lift home?' he asked casually as she was about to cross the road.

'No sardine can tonight.' She laughed. 'Grant has a meeting. But don't worry, thanks, I'll get a bus on the corner.'

'Well, if you can't bear the thought of

sitting in my van, I'll quite understand,' he said, half-seriously, 'but it's parked right here and it's much cleaner inside than you'd think.'

She hesitated. He was only being polite and a lift home would be a lot better than standing on the bus for half an hour. She accepted gratefully and clambered up on to the passenger seat.

Inside, behind the front seats, the van was furnished with built-in cupboards down one side and had a wide bunk across the end.

'Everything except a kitchen sink, I see,' she observed as he started the engine. It sounded a bit asthmatic but caught after the second attempt.

'This van has been everywhere with me,' he said, easing it out into the traffic. 'I wouldn't want to drive anything else.'

She could barely hear him above the noise of the engine, and slid around on the hard, upright seat until she got the knack of holding onto a grip on the door.

'So where else have you been in this van of yours?'

'Before I went to America I took a year off and went across the top of Africa from Morocco to Alexandria,' he said. 'I did quite a bit of mountain climbing there. It's a wonderful, wild country. I met up with some wandering Arabs and followed their route for a bit and really got to know the desert. It was great. I'd like to go back there sometime.'

This man who hated the concrete jungle of New York was quite at home in the rocky wastes far from anywhere. She imagined herself exploring the uninhabited wilds of the North African desert with him.

'How did you manage on your own? What did you eat?' she asked.

'Goat meat, sometimes; but that was considered a delicacy, strictly for high days and holidays.' He smiled. 'Usually I ate vegetables roasted over coals — quite tasty. The women there bake a flat bread on the fire which they serve with every meal. And a sort of porridge made from millet.'

'How on earth did you make yourself understood? Did they speak English?' Andrea was fascinated.

'Not outside the cities, but I had enough Arabic to get around, and by the time I left, I was quite fluent. Being able to speak the language got me out of quite a few tight spots up in the hills.'

Was there nothing this man couldn't do, she thought crossly. Artistic, athletic, and on top of that, fluent in Arabic and goodness knows what other languages.

She stole a look at his face as he drove. His mouth, normally drawn in an uncompromising line, had relaxed into a half-smile as he talked. He's very attractive in a raffish sort of a way, she thought, noticing that his wild, black mane of hair was badly in need of a cut. She had to resist a sudden impulse to smooth back the unruly strands that blew across his face.

All too soon the camper van came to

a noisy halt outside her flat. While she was still struggling with the awkward handle of the door, Luke walked around and opened it for her with a gallant flourish.

'Thanks very much, I hope it wasn't too far out of your way,' she said.

'Not at all. As a matter of fact we're just five minutes away across the park,' he told her cheerfully. 'We moved into a house over there last weekend. Good night, see you tomorrow.'

He drove off and she stood stock-still on the pavement, surprised at the stab of disappointment she felt. 'We'? He'd said, 'We've taken a house'.

She knew he wasn't married, so he must be living with a girlfriend.

Well, what do you expect, she asked herself; no-one like Luke Sullivan would live on his own. His girlfriend must be that gorgeous Hailey in the photograph.

She told herself that it really didn't matter to her what his domestic arrangements were and ran upstairs to tidy the flat before Grant arrived for coffee.

* * *

'So, Pumpkin, tell me all about it,' Grant murmured lazily. Andrea was snuggled next to him on the sofa, her head on his shoulder. 'How was your day and how was your terrible boss?'

'He's not so bad, really,' she said, considering. 'He's actually quite human when he's talking about the job. But he's made it quite clear that he thinks I'm an idiot who can't be trusted to do anything without asking him first. He actually seems to resent the fact that I'm a woman, and that I'm there at all.'

'My poor baby. Well, you can't say you weren't warned.'

'Although I have to admit I've learned a lot from him already,' she added.

'Mm. So what are you busy with?' he asked, drawing her closer to him. 'What sort of work are you going to be doing with him? Anything exciting?'

'Well, the most fabulous thing happened yesterday. Tweedledum and Tweedledee were in seventh heaven because we've been given this enormous account that's going to totally change our lives . . . '
She broke off abruptly, remembering too late the warning from Luke about idle talk.

'So . . . what is it? What's this big new account?'

'Oh — well — it's for United Northern Insurance,' she mumbled, feeling like a traitor. Darn it, don't be silly, she thought. This is Grant, remember?

'Are you sure?' He straightened up. 'How on earth did that happen? Everyone knew they were unhappy with their old agency and our art department put forward a really good campaign to them but didn't get anywhere. And now your titchy little agency has been given their business? That's incredible!'

'Not so incredible,' said Andrea, stung. 'We're not that bad. Besides, we've got Luke with us now and I guess they like his work.'

'That's probably it,' mused Grant. 'He must have done some work for them before and they're just taking their account to wherever he is. Well, well, well. Aren't you the lucky ones? I wonder how long they'll stay with you? I mean, let's face it, even now you've got the famous Luke Sullivan working there, your whole outfit is pretty one-horse. You aren't geared to cope with TV adverts and national campaigns.'

'We soon will be if Luke has anything to do with it,' answered Andrea sharply. She hadn't expected him to be so interested in her news, and wished now that she hadn't told him, but it was too late. Anyway, word would have got out sooner or later, and it wasn't as if she would tell him anything about the actual campaign.

'Like some more coffee?' she asked.

'No, thanks.' He settled back with a contented sigh and began planting gentle little kisses on her cheek.

Being with Grant is so comfortable

when he's like this, she thought dreamily. This feels really nice. I'm glad he agreed to stay in for once.

'So, let's talk about our plans for the weekend,' he murmured.

'We're going to see Barbara on Saturday, remember?' she said. 'Otherwise, nothing much. We could go for a walk on Sunday, if you like. What have you got in mind?'

'I thought we might go down to Springfield to visit my mother,' he said casually. 'It's time the two of you met, don't you think?'

Her heart leapt. All of a sudden he sounded serious about her. Meeting the mother was usually a signal of some sort, wasn't it?

'Sounds nice. Would I have to dress up?' she teased, lifting her face to his and returning his kisses in between her words.

'Definitely your best bib-and-tucker,' he answered, drawing back and looking at her seriously. 'I'd like you to make a good impression on Mother. She's a darling, but she's a bit old-fashioned about things like dressing for meals. I thought we could go down on Saturday after tea and come back after lunch on Sunday. That will give you time to get to know each other.'

Oh horrors, thought Andrea. Dress for meals? I bet there'll be a whole tableful of family silver and if I pick up the wrong knife, I'll be doomed for life in the eyes of his mother.

Andrea had always known that Grant came from a well-to-do family but had never thought much about it. But now, his previous references to the library in his mother's home, his school holidays spent skiing in Austria or Switzerland, and the fact that he'd been given his first sports car on his eighteenth birthday, began to make her feel uneasy.

Stories that she'd read about week-ends in country houses came back to her. What if there's a maid who insists on unpacking my clothes? She'll see that I sleep in my brother's old T-shirt! I haven't even a proper weekend case, only that backpack I used at college. And would she be expected to tip the staff?

Anxious queries flitted through her mind as she lay against Grant's shoulder.

'Don't look so worried, silly.' He kissed her again. 'Mother's going to love you on sight. Wear that tartan outfit of yours; you look stunning in that.'

'All right,' she said slowly, 'but if I go there dressed to kill when I'm meant to be having a casual weekend, your mother's going to get quite the wrong impression of me.'

'You can hardly wear what you normally wear on a Sunday,' he replied sharply. 'T-shirts and jeans won't go down well at Applethorpe House, sweetie, so leave them behind. My mother hates to see women in trousers of any sort. She has pretty high standards and I'd hate it if you didn't measure up to them.'

Suddenly Andrea wasn't looking forward to the weekend at all.

* * *

Barbara and Grant were getting on famously. From the moment he walked into her flat that Saturday afternoon, the two of them had been talking non-stop, laughing together like old friends.

Andrea was delighted. She'd been a bit worried that they wouldn't click. Sometimes Grant could be a bit stand-offish when he met people for the first time. But here he was, chatting animatedly while Barbara prepared the tea and poured it for them, helping himself to two of her home-made biscuits and congratulating her on her baking skills.

'The looks of an angel and you can bake, too!' he enthused. 'What a talented lady. Can't you teach Andy how to make biscuits like these?'

Barbara was beaming at him.

91

It turned out that years before, she had actually worked with some of the advertising people that Grant knew. He plied her with questions about her work as a photographer before her accident, swapping stories about magazine editors and other mutual acquaintances.

For her part she asked just the right sort of intelligent questions to get him talking about his work, while Andrea relaxed and listened, pleased that her two favourite people were getting along so well together.

'Of course,' Grant was saying, 'I work terribly long hours but it's worth it in the end. For instance, I've just had a group of delightful Japanese clients to keep happy, and when they left they gave us a very nice slice of their advertising account — over half a million pounds for starters, and if they like our stuff, they'll increase their budget next year.'

'Why, Grant, you never told me that!' exclaimed Andrea. 'That's wonderful for you! Congratulations!'

'That's nothing. Tell Barbara about your coup with United Northern Insurance, Andrea.'

Andrea told Barbara about the new account and all the exciting work that lay ahead for her.

'What's the theme of your campaign going to be — any ideas yet?' asked Grant. 'Or is the terrible Luke playing his cards very close to his chest? I don't suppose he'll let you have a look-in until it's all settled and approved.'

'Probably not,' she agreed equably, not wanting to discuss it with Grant.

Privately she hoped that if she could come up with a good enough suggestion for the campaign, Luke would take her ideas seriously.

'How are you and Luke getting along these days?' queried Barbara.

'Better, I suppose. You know, Barbs, before he came I had this picture in my mind of some smooth operator, very sophisticated and full of himself — but he's not like that at all. He's quite the opposite and looks more like a farmer than a media man. He even comes to work in old jeans!'

'The two of you should get on pretty well then,' said Grant sharply. 'But enough about him. How about another cup of tea for a thirsty man?'

All too soon it was time for Andrea and Grant to set off on their drive to the village of Springfield where Grant's mother lived.

'I refuse to say goodbye, Barbara, because I know we're going to be seeing a lot more of each other,' said Grant as they left her flat. 'So I'll just say *au revoir*.' And he kissed her hand with a self-mocking bow.

'Cheerio for now,' said Barbara, laughing. 'I've really enjoyed meeting you. Andy must bring you to supper one evening soon.'

'A very nice girl,' he said approvingly as he and Andrea roared off out of town. 'And clever, too. She's really kept up with what's going on in the world. Someone in her position could easily become a bit of a recluse.'

'She's still rather shy about meeting new people, though,' said Andrea. 'I'm really glad the two of you got on so well.'

'You didn't tell me how pretty she is,' he commented.

'She is, isn't she? And she's such a lovely person. Since my sister, Annabelle, got married and went to Australia, Barbara's probably the closest friend I've got here in Lymchester. I tell her all my problems.'

'Hey, I thought you told *me* everything,' he protested. 'Isn't my shoulder wide enough for you?'

'Silly,' she murmured, 'I can't tell you everything. Besides, sometimes *you're* the problem!'

He laughed, sounding quite pleased.

'I have to keep you on your toes,' he said smugly. 'It doesn't do to let a woman think she can have it all her own way.'

Andrea was momentarily taken aback. How could Grant talk to her like that, as if she was part of some huge army of females all dying to have their way with him? But maybe that's what she was, she thought bleakly, thinking about all those glamorous secretaries that he had at his beck and call all day.

But if that was the case then why was he taking her to meet his mother?

★ ★ ★

By the time they drove through the gates of Applethorpe House, she had recovered her good humour. It was an imposing, red-brick building at the end of a gravel driveway, and was surrounded by green lawns edged with flower beds.

As they came to a halt near the big front door, a slender figure straightened up from behind the rose bushes and waved.

'Grant, darling!' His mother carefully put down her gardening fork and took off her gloves as she came unhurriedly towards the car. 'And you must be Andrea. How nice to meet you.'

She smiled briefly at Andrea, who

was still struggling to get out of the car, and turned back to Grant.

'How was your journey, my dear? Traffic not too bad, I hope? Bring your bags in and show Andrea her room. I'm sure she'd like a little wash before we have a drink.'

As Grant lifted her bag from the back of the car, Andrea was miserably aware of how cheap and new her little red case looked.

Oh well, she thought, as she followed him and his mother into the house, Mrs Carter will just have to take me as I am.

★   ★   ★

The weekend was every bit as bad as Andrea had feared, but not in the way she'd expected. Far from having lots of servants, Mrs Carter had no help at all in the house these days, but this didn't mean she had let her standards slip.

'I'm quite able to look after things myself. Goodness me, one woman all on her own can surely be expected to manage a little housework,' she demurred when Andrea complimented her on her home.

Upstairs, Andrea had counted five bedrooms and hadn't even ventured up to the floor above.

Now they were sitting in front of the fire in the sitting-room. Gold silk cushions were scattered over the pale cream sofas and a silver bowl of pink roses glowed softly on a highly polished coffee table. Everything was spotless in the immaculate room, including their hostess.

Mrs Carter had changed into a grey woollen dress that she wore with a mohair stole around her shoulders, and as she sipped her sherry she eyed her son fondly.

'Grant's been doing so well in his career, hasn't he, Andrea?' she said proudly. 'Don't be surprised if he becomes president of Mattler Horne one day!'

'Er — no, I won't be, Mrs Carter,' answered Andrea, stifling a giggle. She tried to catch Grant's eye to share the humour, but he wouldn't look at her. Grant was, after all, only a very junior executive, and for all his talk of winning a lot of business from the Japanese industrialists, she knew he wasn't in charge of that account.

The fact that he was answerable to Gordon Forbes, a senior partner at Mattler Horne, annoyed him, and he often grumbled to Andrea about not being given enough authority to make decisions. Not that he'd mentioned this when he was talking to Barbara. Or to his mother, apparently.

It sounded as if Mrs Carter thought her son was practically running the company. Well, Andrea wouldn't disillusion her.

'By the way, have you had a call from my cousin Stanley? Stanley Beaumont?' asked Mrs Carter, turning to Grant with a roguish look in her eye.

'No, why do you ask?'

'Well, my dear, he's just been appointed as the new chairman of Fastabank and I think he might have good reason to call you soon. But I won't spoil his little surprise.'

'Mother! Do you mean he's going to give me Fastabank's advertising business?'

Mrs Carter smiled prettily and looked down at her hands. 'My dear, my lips are sealed. Let's just say I know you'll be pleased with what he has to say.'

'Oh, Mother, you're a marvel.' Grant chuckled with delight. 'He's going to give me their advertising account, isn't he? That's wonderful. I can't tell you what a lot that will mean to me. It will give me a really big account of my own. That'll be a shot in the eye for old Forbes.'

'Now, Grant, I haven't said a word. Don't jump to conclusions. The subject is closed.'

Mother and son exchanged conspiratorial smiles and Mrs Carter turned to Andrea.

'So, Andrea, tell me about yourself. Where were you educated?'

'In Scotland. I went to our local school, where my mother taught history.'

'Really?' she murmured. 'And after that?'

'I went to art college in Edinburgh.'

'How nice,' said Grant's mother, obviously unimpressed.

An awkward silence fell. Casting around for something to say, Andrea noticed a small wooden chest in the corner of the room.

'That's a beautiful little chest — is it an antique?' she asked.

'It is sweet, isn't it?' agreed Mrs Carter. 'Yes, it belonged to Grant's grandfather, but it's not really of any value. I just keep it for sentiment. Most of the pieces in this room date back to the eighteenth century so they need quite a bit of tender loving care. Especially the carpet. It's a genuine Bokhara and I've been assured it's over three hundred years old.' Her laugh tinkled. 'Of course, one of these days I shall hand over responsibility for the house to Grant's bride, whoever she may be. Until that day, I regard it as my duty to keep all these lovely things as beautiful as when they were new.'

Andrea swallowed and glanced across at Grant, who was smiling happily back at her.

'Andrea loves beautiful things, don't you, Andy? She's quite a little artist. I told you she works in an advertising studio, didn't I, Mother?'

'You did, darling. Well then, I'm sure you'll enjoy looking at some of our treasures here at Applethorpe, Andrea. You must ask Grant to show you round.'

With that, Mrs Carter rose gracefully. 'There are just a few little things to do in the kitchen. Grant, darling, you look after — er — Andrea. Offer her another sherry, if she wants one. Dinner will be served in ten minutes.'

'Can't I give you a hand in the kitchen, Mrs Carter?' offered Andrea, but was cut short.

'Of course not, my dear, you're a

visitor. I wouldn't dream of it.'

'Mother's marvellous,' said Grant after she'd left the room. 'While I was growing up we had a household staff of three — and a gardener, of course — but when my father died she decided to do everything herself. She said she was tired of servants who kept breaking things and didn't do a proper job, and anyway, she enjoys keeping busy.'

'Wouldn't she rather do something else — work for charity for instance?' queried Andrea, thinking of her own mother.

Retired for some years, her mum was busier now than she had ever been while teaching, and Andrea often joked that she had to phone her at midnight if she wanted to be sure of finding her at home. She was involved in almost everything that went on in her village and, what with her pottery lessons and quilting classes and her on-going love affair with two big Labradors, her mother's house wasn't always very tidy. But it was much more comfortable to live in than this one, she thought.

'Our home is very important to both of us and Mother really enjoys looking after it,' said Grant. 'Of course, she's keeping it nice for me. One day I'll be expected to take over the running of Applethorpe, but until then Mother keeps it perfect. And it is a lovely home, don't you think?'

'Yes,' she answered faintly.

'But that's enough about the house.'

He moved across to sit on the arm of her chair and started to kiss her very passionately.

'Careful!' she giggled. 'You'll mess up my hair, and then your mother will guess what we've been up to.'

He drew back instantly. 'Here's my comb,' he said. 'We don't want her to get ideas.'

'Whyever not? Does she think we've just met?'

'Don't be silly, Pumpkin, but you're right — it just doesn't seem the right thing to do in Mother's house.'

'For goodness sake', we're just

kissing! It's not as if we're going in for a full-scale orgy!'

'There's no need to be vulgar.'

Hurt, she sat stiffly upright until, five minutes later, they heard the tinkle of a bell.

'Ah, dinner,' Grant exclaimed with relief. 'Let's see what splendid meal Mother has cooked in your honour.'

He ushered Andrea through to the dining-room where a long, lace-covered table gleamed in the light of silver candelabra.

Grant's mother served three exquisite courses from silver dishes placed on the sideboard. Everything she did was done precisely and without fuss, and while they talked she removed the dirty plates, served the next course and passed the wine, all without any interruption.

She was the most efficient woman Andrea had ever met.

How did she ever manage to cook this delicious food, set the table, keep this huge house clean and still find time to work in the garden? She must be some sort of superwoman, thought Andrea. Never mind me trying to impress Grant's mother, she's certainly impressing me!

Again, her offer to help — this time with the washing-up — was politely declined, and when she went up to bed she found a vase of roses on her bedside table and a hot-water bottle tucked under the covers.

Lying between the crisply-ironed linen sheets, Andrea felt a slow depression settle on her. Apart from that brief moment before dinner, Grant had more or less ignored her the whole evening.

Instead, he'd given his mother his full attention, telling her about his work and his life in town in general.

His mother had listened, as if transfixed, to his every word, laughing at all his witty comments, and neither of them had made any attempt to include her in the conversation.

Andrea had found herself feeling

embarrassed. In the setting of his mother's house, it was as if Grant had become a different person, exaggerating all his stories to make himself the most important figure in every anecdote he told her.

★   ★   ★

Next morning, Andrea was determined to get to know Mrs Carter a little better. After all, that was the whole point of the weekend. She rose early and dressed in a pale-blue skirt and a cream silk blouse.

It was such a lovely day outside, she thought ruefully, looking out of her bedroom window at the rolling, green hills stretching out beyond the high, grey walls of Applethorpe.

She wished she could just pull on her tracksuit and go for a quick run before breakfast. Instead, she slipped on her high-heeled pumps and went downstairs to find her hostess. But again all her offers to help were coolly rebuffed.

Mrs Carter had already laid the table for breakfast.

'I'm very well organised, thank you, Andrea. Anyway, I wouldn't want you to spoil that pretty little outfit. My goodness, you young things wear your skirts so short these days, don't you? Of course, if you're particularly hungry, you could start with your cereal now, but I think we really ought to wait for Grant. I'll just let him sleep in a bit longer as he works so hard. Why don't you just take a walk around the garden? Or, if you like, the Sunday papers have arrived; they're in the sitting-room.'

Andrea opted for reading the papers in the sitting-room, and as she did so, the house was completely silent around her except for the ticking of the grandfather clock in the hall. Wherever Mrs Carter was, and whatever she was doing, she had made it perfectly clear that she didn't want Andrea under her efficient little feet.

So much for getting to know each other, she thought grimly, trying to turn the pages quietly. It was a great relief when she heard Grant's noisy descent from his bedroom and they could go in to breakfast. It was nearly ten o'clock. She was starving.

★ ★ ★

Driving home that afternoon, Grant hummed cheerfully to himself.

'Well, I think that went off quite well, don't you? What do you think of Mother? Don't you think she's amazing?'

'Yes,' said Andrea truthfully. 'I don't know how she does it. But I got the feeling that she's not all that keen on me.'

'Nonsense,' he said fondly. 'You know what mothers are like. Nobody is ever good enough for their sons, and all that. Don't worry. I'm sure she liked you. How could she not like my sweet little Pumpkin?'

'Grant, I wish you wouldn't call me that,' she said crossly, shaking off his arm. She was suddenly impatient with his nickname for her. 'It makes me feel — oh, I don't know — fat.'

'Well, you're not exactly a bag of bones, are you?' he answered, giving her a critical look. 'Come to think of it, you could easily lose a few pounds. Thin women always wear their clothes better — look at Mother. But I won't call you Pumpkin any more if you don't like it.'

She stared out of the window, barely holding back the tears that threatened to spill down her cheeks. The weekend had not been a wild success and now Grant was starting to criticise her again. I expect it's all my fault, she thought bleakly. I'm just the wrong sort of person for Mrs Carter, and no matter what I do, she's never going to approve of me. Maybe I'm just the wrong sort of girl for Grant.

Unwilling to pursue that line of thought, she spent the remainder of the journey mentally turning over ideas for the United Northern campaign.

A Great Idea

Andrea yawned. It was half-past one, definitely time for a break, and she'd been working on the computer non-stop since eight that morning without so much as a cup of coffee.

She and Luke had been mulling over various ideas for three days now, and they still hadn't got very far with the United Northern campaign.

They worked silently, the studio littered with pamphlets extolling the virtues of the different insurance packages offered by their new client, who wanted a campaign that would cover the whole range.

Andrea had made a collection of every advertisement that she could find for rival insurance companies, clipping them from financial magazines and papers.

'Good idea,' Luke said approvingly,

'that way we'll have some sort of idea of what the opposition is doing.'

'That's why I did it,' she answered him pertly — really, did the man think she was a complete idiot? 'But every idea that I come up with seems to have already been thought of before. Everything I do seems to end up looking like one of these. Serious men in serious suits warning you of serious trouble if you don't insure with their company. Seriously boring!'

'Well, it must work or they wouldn't stick with that format,' Luke reasoned. 'Did you know you've got ink on your nose?'

'Seriously?' she quipped, looking up at him.

'Not too serious. It looks kind of cute.'

I've got to stop catching his eye like that, she thought, flushing. Every time she did, a hot current surged through her whole body. The man was undeniably attractive and she couldn't help being aware that he found her so as well. I bet he has this effect on every woman he meets, she thought crossly. Well, this is one woman who's able to ignore all those macho good looks and rough charm. I've got Grant.

She decided to read the client profile once again. Sixty-seven percent of United Northern customers were women . . . well, what appealed to women? She stared ahead and suddenly she said, 'Babies! Let's use babies instead of men in suits.'

As she spoke she had the most marvellous picture in her mind of babies dressed up in miniature suits, discussing business. Babies banging on tables and shuffling bits of paper around, advising each other to use United Northern. Babies speaking with deep, businesslike voices on the TV spots.

Her words tumbled out as she tried to explain her idea to Luke.

'Toddlers!' she blurted. 'We dress them up in three-piece suits and put them in an office and take lots of photos of them. Then we choose the best shots and put sort of cartoon bubbles of their words coming out of their mouths. It could work fantastically well! People would be so surprised to see these babies that they'd just have to read the whole advert!'

Luke looked at her and shook his head. 'Just like a woman,' he mocked. 'Babies on the brain from the time you were born. You're all the same.'

'Don't patronise me!' she flashed back at him. 'Listen! For the TV shots we use the same babies pretending to have a meeting, and we use voice-overs to make them sound like elderly men. Luke, it could work! It could have a lot of impact! It could be such fun!'

'I don't think a 'fun' campaign is quite what United Northern had in mind,' he said slowly. 'I'm not saying it couldn't work . . . hmm, maybe you're not just a pretty face after all.'

'I'll ignore that remark,' she said, swept along by her enthusiasm. 'Just think: we could put spectacles on their noses and . . . oh, it could be fantastic!'

'I've worked with babies before on a

shoot for baby food,' muttered Luke. 'They're awful. You sit for hours in the studio and you're lucky if you get two decent shots. The rest of the time the baby is crying or having its nappy changed or having its bottle. A whole lot of babies together would be a nightmare. But it's not a bad idea.'

Andrea's eyes sparkled, her mind racing ahead. 'We'd have to get the little suits made specially. And where would we get the babies?'

'From a model agency. Where else would they find all those cute toothless little things on baby cereal boxes? Finding the babies won't be a problem. Let's get Martin in and discuss it with him — he'll be the one doing the still shots.'

Then suddenly it was all happening. The photographer left his darkroom to come across to the studio, and over coffee they discussed exactly how they'd go about setting up the shots.

They decided that they'd need six babies, none older than two years.

Martin phoned an agency right there and then, booking them for a week's time.

'Andy, your first job is to organise the little suits to be made as soon as possible,' ordered Luke. 'Phone the model agency and check the sizes of the babies first, then see if you can find a theatrical costumier to make the suits, and if you can't, then get a tailor. But they're going to have to move fast on this. Once you've found someone to make the suits then you'll need to go out and buy all the props we're going to need, like spectacles and maybe a gavel for the chairman to bang on the table; notebooks, pens and so on.'

Andrea felt quite breathless just listening to all this. Her idea had been taken up and was being carried along at a dizzy rate.

'What do I use for money?'

'Ask at reception for some petty cash, of course,' he snapped irritably. 'What do you normally do?'

'I don't normally do this sort of thing

at all,' she retorted. 'But I'm willing to if I'm asked nicely.'

Luke glared at her and she stared back defiantly. No matter how caught up in his arrangements he might be, she wasn't going to let him start ordering her about. After all, it had been her idea.

To her surprise, he grinned and looked at her with something close to approval. Then he stood up and bowed, doffing an imaginary hat.

'My apologies, your majesty! Would you be able to find time to do a few favours for your humble servant? A visit to a tailor perhaps? A few phone calls?'

'When I'm asked like that, kind sir, how can I refuse? I would deem it a pleasure,' she answered, smiling in spite of herself.

'Right, that's settled then.' He turned his attention back to the photographer. 'Martin, let's see what we can do about the office scenery. We might have to hire some; let's go and look at your studio.'

The two men went off together and

Jeannie looked admiringly at Andrea.

'Wow, I thought he was going to bite your head off! You've got a nerve!'

'Not really,' she answered slowly. Even though he'd seemed to mock her when she protested, his look of respect had not been lost on her. I've found the way to handle him, she thought, and suddenly the thought of working with him seemed a lot more attractive.

'When he gets going, he certainly gets going!' said Jeannie.

'Gets bossy, you mean,' answered Andrea. 'I see what they mean about him ordering people about.'

But he had liked her idea! They were actually going to use her idea for the campaign!

* * *

The following week passed in a blurry haze of work. Andrea and Jeannie were still busy with the computer graphics course three evenings a week, and during the day. Andrea rushed around with lists of things to get for the shoot. She had no luck finding a local theatrical costumier, but after trying three tailors, she found one prepared to do a rush job and who would make the little suits immediately.

She tracked down some tiny spectacles at a novelty shop and cajoled an office equipment business to hire out some smart furniture for the day.

Martin had decided it would be a good idea if he worked together with Joe Askew, the film maker Luke was going to use for the TV spot. If they had all the babies together in one room, they had to make the most of it.

By Wednesday evening, Martin's photo studio looked like a very smart office, with an oak desk and six matching chairs. Notebooks, a telephone, and a leather desk-set completed the illusion.

The little suits had arrived, and at the last minute Luke had suggested that the babies should all wear matching green ties embroidered with the logo of United Northern.

Martin surveyed his studio, which was filled with all these props.

'I hope you haven't mentioned this idea to anyone, Andy,' Martin said as he checked that all was in order for the shoot the following day. 'I've got a feeling this is going to be a hot campaign.'

'Don't worry, even the tailor didn't know he was making the little suits for an advertisement. He thought they were dressing-up clothes for a nursery school. The poor man thought I was a really crazy teacher, paying out all that money for toddlers' toys!' giggled Andrea.

'He's a lucky man! His clothes are about to become famous throughout the nation,' said Martin. 'But we can't tell him beforehand. We don't want any other advertising agency to get wind of what we're going to be doing.'

'Well, you needn't worry,' she retorted. 'Luke's paranoid about secrecy and has drummed that in to us already.'

She was actually feeling very pleased with how discreet she'd been about the campaign. Although she'd been bursting to tell him, she hadn't breathed a word of this idea to Grant during the past week. In fact, the only person she'd told had been Barbara, but she knew Barbara would say nothing and besides, she saw almost no-one to talk to apart from Andrea herself.

'I can't believe we're actually going to do this,' she remarked happily to Luke as they descended in the lift together that evening. 'Suddenly one of my crazy notions is turning into something really big!'

'The best ideas always happen in a flash.' He looked down at her, smiling at her enthusiasm. 'I think this one could be a winner.'

'Do you really?' She was unable to suppress the excitement which was bubbling out of her. 'Oh, Luke, I hope it works out.'

'It will, Andy. Martin knows exactly what we want; he's completely on our wavelength. And Joe's a good film man; I've used him before in London. We won't be disappointed.'

She noticed with pleasure that he said 'our' wavelength. They sounded like a team.

'What's that you've got there? Overtime?' he asked, looking at the folder under her arm.

'Oh — it's just some rough layouts for the United Northern newspaper adverts,' she told him, blushing. 'I wanted to play around with them tonight. You know those smaller ones that we were planning for the financial weeklies? I thought I could improve the layouts a bit. Maybe find a snappier caption.'

'Don't overdo it. We're going to be busy enough tomorrow. You'd do better to get an early night. Actually, Andy, how about having a drink with me before you go home?'

'Oh, I'd love to! But I'm sorry, I have to meet someone.'

She was genuinely regretful. She would have welcomed the chance to cement this new-found rapport with her new boss.

His face tightened at her refusal.

'Oh, of course, the sardine can,' he said. 'Then don't let me keep you.'

Honestly, she thought with a flash of irritation, I'm not going to explain my every move to him. Does he think I do nothing but see Grant every night? But he just can't miss the chance to have a dig at Grant's sports car. If he's that jealous of it, why doesn't he buy a decent car for himself? I'm sure he could afford it.

Andrea hurried down the street to the Chinese takeaway before heading for Barbara's flat.

As she'd expected, her friend had been delighted for her when she'd first told her that the agency were going to use her idea for the insurance company campaign.

Since then, she'd kept Barbara up to date with everything she was doing to prepare for the shoot. Barbara was a good listener, and with all her photographic experience she had contributed a few useful tips about filming babies.

'Don't try to get them to do anything for longer than about three minutes at a time,' she'd advised. 'Let them wander all over the place. The minute you try to put toddlers where you want them, that's exactly where they don't want to be. Just let Martin and Joe follow them around with the cameras. Oh, and give the mothers a nice cup of tea and keep them out of sight — they're often more trouble than the babies!'

That evening, Andrea and Barbara had just finished their chicken with cashew nuts when there was a knock at the door.

'Who could that be at this time?' Barbara wondered. 'I bet it's someone selling something. Could you get it, Andy?'

Andrea went to the door and opened it, polite words of refusal already forming on her lips but, to her surprise, it was Grant who stood there.

'Oh — Andy — hi,' he said in some confusion, and then added hurriedly, 'I thought I'd find you here so I took a chance and just came round. Is it OK if I come in?'

'Of course,' Barbara called from the sitting-room. 'I'm delighted you've found your way here again. Come in.'

'Oh, you've eaten already.' He sounded so forlorn when he surveyed the remains of their meal that Andrea laughed.

'Barbara won't mind if I make you cheese on toast or something on those lines, will you, Barbs?'

'Of course not, you carry on. And I'll make coffee for all of us.'

'How was work today, Grant?' Andrea enquired, slicing cheese on to bread and putting it under the grill.

'Quite horrible,' he said crossly. 'Old man Forbes is really getting on my nerves. The man's impossible. I think I might look around for something else, actually. Mattler Horne are not the only agency in the world.'

'Oh, Grant, what happened?' she asked, her heart sinking.

Ever since she'd met Grant he'd been talking of leaving Mattler Horne and

125

going to London. He was convinced that that was where his abilities would be most appreciated.

The last place Andrea wanted to live was London, but if Grant really moved away then she'd be forced to make some sort of decision. She couldn't bear the thought of seeing him only at weekends, but neither did she want to think of leaving Lymchester — especially not now, with her work becoming so interesting and having just moved into her lovely new flat.

But if she stayed behind while he went to the city, Andrea knew their relationship might not stand the separation. She could lose him to the bright lights for ever, and she couldn't bear the thought of that either.

'The silly old fool ticked me off in front of a whole roomful of people at a staff meeting,' he fumed. 'He gave me a real row about the way I handle my expense account — I ask you! I'm given such a miserable allowance as it is, but I'm expected to entertain clients all the time — take them to lunch and buy them drinks. If it wasn't for the fact I was so darned nice to those Japanese businessmen then we'd never have won their account.'

'That's not fair at all,' she sympathised. 'But don't let him get you down; not when you're doing so well.'

'You know, Grant may be right, maybe it is time for him to move on,' Barbara put in suddenly. 'Sometimes an ambitious person like yourself becomes stale in one job and you need a change. And in advertising it's often the quickest way to move up the ladder. People get jealous and block a talented person when they look as though they're getting ahead. Your next position might be as a senior executive and a big improvement all round.'

'Barbara understands my position exactly.' Grant smiled gratefully at the blind girl. 'Old Forbes takes the credit for everything I do and I don't think I'm getting anywhere. I'm going to have a serious talk with him tomorrow and if things don't change, then I'll resign. There are plenty of other agencies who'll snap me up.'

Dismayed, Andrea served the toasted cheese in silence, curling up on the sofa next to Grant and watching him while he ate. Sensing that he had found a sympathetic ally, he directed most of his comments towards Barbara for the rest of the evening, and he expounded at length on what he'd done since he joined Mattler Horne, how many customers he had lured into the firm with a combination of his own charm and intelligence, how valuable he was to the firm, and how badly they would miss him when he resigned.

Andrea listened, hardly able to believe what she was hearing. Did Grant really see himself as so important? She knew his actual position in the agency, and in the months since she'd started going out with him he'd often complained that he was never given enough responsibility to prove his worth.

Yet here he was giving Barbara the impression that he was the kingpin of the whole company.

Suddenly she felt impatient listening to his complaints and stood up.

'It's getting late. I'll have to go; I have a heavy day tomorrow.'

She expected Grant to get up, too, and to offer her a lift home, but he simply turned to her and said, 'What, already? It's only nine o'clock. The night is young. Is there any more coffee where that came from, Barbara?'

'Of course,' said Barbara. 'Sit there, and I'll make us all another cup.'

'Not for me, I really must be off.' Andrea walked uncertainly to the door. 'I'll catch the bus, then, shall I?'

'Right, I'll give you a call tomorrow,' Grant said lazily from the sofa.

'Don't worry about him,' said Barbara soothingly as she walked with Andrea to the door. 'He just needs someone to listen to him while he gets it off his chest. I think he's really upset. You go on home. I'll have a talk with him and try to get him to see things in a more reasonable light.'

Andrea was annoyed as she walked to the bus stop. Perhaps Grant did need to talk it out with someone else besides herself; perhaps he knew that she wouldn't listen to his exaggerations and half-truths very sympathetically. But how could he just go on sitting on Barbara's sofa like that, ignoring Andrea and letting her go home on the bus? Wasn't she someone special in his life, or would just any willing female do when he needed sympathy? And how could her friend be taken in by all his rubbish?

The more she thought about it, the more annoyed she became with them both. However, by the time she reached her flat she was in a calmer mood, and as she started thinking about the photo shoot the following morning, Grant's problems faded into the background.

I'm just too tired to do anything much on those layouts, she decided, and then realised she'd left the folder at Barbara's flat.

That settled it. She ran a hot bath which she sprinkled liberally with scented bath salts. This was her favourite way to unwind and she luxuriated in the fragrant warmth for nearly half an hour.

Her last thoughts before she fell into a deep sleep were that Grant would probably change his mind about resigning. This was just another of his bad moods and it would pass, as his bad moods always did.

Hectic Times!

It was going to work. After a long morning spent with toddlers crying, gurgling, smiling and shrieking, she knew her idea was going to work.

They looked so sweet dressed in their little suits, and when she and Jeannie put them on the office chairs, the first thing they did was stand up and try to climb on to the table. They chewed the notepads, threw the telephone on to the floor and generally caused mayhem. One little boy, a wicked little charmer of about eighteen months, took off his glasses and examined them gravely, then tried to push them back on his nose.

'Beautiful, kid! Do it again,' said Joe, following the children around, his video camera hoisted on his shoulder, filming everything they did.

Martin's camera flashed non-stop

and he was delighted when two of the babies started pushing each other in the chest.

'That's good,' he muttered. 'Now put those pamphlets down and let's see what they do with them.'

Andrea spread the United Northern pamphlets across the table and the babies obliged by picking them up and waving them around wildly before giving them a good chewing.

At the end of two hours, Joe signalled that he was satisfied with the footage he had, which was just as well because the babies were turning crotchety and were no longer interested in the biscuits Jeannie offered them whenever tears threatened.

'Time to go home!' said Andrea, and picked up one little boy whose lower lip was trembling and who was on the point of tears. Andrea began humming a nursery song to him, swinging him gently from side to side, and was rewarded with a big watery smile.

'Where's Mummy, then? Let's go and

find her,' she said and, turning, bumped into Luke who was watching her with an odd expression.

'Have you finished here?' he queried.

'Yes, I think so. The babies have, at any rate; they're very tired.'

Luke had a pen in his hand, and the toddler in her arms grabbed it, put it firmly in his mouth, and gave it an experimental bite.

'Only a few teeth but he knows what to do with them!' he commented ruefully. 'Hmm. Enjoyed today, have you, Andy? Babies suit you. I suppose it's just a matter of time before you'll be off to have some of your own.'

'Well, I certainly hope to have children one day,' she said, cuddling the little boy and pulling a face at him, 'but it won't be for a long while yet!'

'That's the trouble with women, no commitment to their jobs. One look at a baby and you all get broody.' He glowered at her. 'Well, you've been working full-time for five years now — I don't expect it'll be long before you start hearing wedding bells and pack up and leave.'

Her jaw dropped. The sheer, galling effrontery of the man!

'For your information, I've no intention of leaving or getting married or having a baby in the foreseeable future. You're stuck with me for a long time yet.'

'Good,' he said.

What did that remark mean, she wondered.

'You've still got a lot of living to do, is what I meant,' he said, reading her thoughts. 'So don't let the driver of the sardine can persuade you otherwise.'

'My relationship with Grant is none of your business.'

'I'm just taking an interest in your well-being.' He grinned. 'Like all the best bosses are supposed to do.'

'The best bosses are polite to the people they work with,' she retorted.

'I'm not so bad, am I?' he asked innocently. 'Isn't life more interesting when I'm around? Come on, how many babies did you get to cuddle before I got here?'

'You are such an — an egotist!' she hissed. 'Life was a lot less complicated before you came.'

'Ah, but less fun; you've practically admitted it!'

He winked at her and went off whistling, leaving her glaring at his retreating back.

* * *

Once the babies were safely dispatched home with their mothers, Andrea, Luke and Martin went across to Joe's video studio and settled down with big mugs of coffee to view the footage he'd filmed that morning.

Joe certainly knew what he was doing when it came to photographing babies. He'd caught them making just the right expressions for the advert and — viewing the film without any sound — it looked hilarious.

'Look at that one with the glasses; it's

as if he's really going to say something important when he takes them off like that,' said Andrea. 'And when they're all bashing those pamphlets, they could be saying something like 'Nothing but United Northern will do for us'.'

'This is great stuff! There's a lot of material here that we can use,' said Luke. 'Excellent work, Joe! Martin, can we see the stills first thing?'

'I'll print them overnight,' Martin promised.

* * *

Before going home that evening, Andrea popped in to see Barbara, buying some chicken pies on the way. She needed to share the success of the day with her friend, but she also wanted to find out what had happened with Grant after she'd left the previous evening.

'I'll swap you a hot pie for something cool to drink.' She sighed, sinking into one of Barbara's easy chairs. 'What a day!'

'Good or bad?'

'Definitely good,' she said. 'The babies were wonderful. They did all the cute things they were supposed to do and everything went off really well.'

'Who's writing the words they're supposed to say?' asked Barbara, putting the pies on to plates and feeling expertly in the fridge for the makings of a salad.

'Luke's writing the copy. There's nothing he can't do,' Andrea admitted, growing silent as she went over the events of the day in her head.

Her mixed-up feelings for the man must have shown in her voice, and Barbara picked up on it at once.

'Oh? What's this I hear?' she teased. 'Is this just admiration or could it be the beginnings of something more serious?'

'Of course not,' Andrea answered indignantly. 'It's just that he's incredibly good at what he does and he's teaching me such a lot. He's insufferably conceited though.'

'Methinks the lady doth protest too much.'

Andrea heard the smiling disbelief in her friend's voice, but although she couldn't escape the fact that she liked Luke a lot more than she should, she wasn't going to admit it to Barbara or anyone else. Not even to herself. She'd just have to ignore the electricity that seemed to spark between them.

'So, how long did Grant stay after I left last night?' she asked casually. 'I'm sorry he was so depressed. Did he finish off all your coffee?'

Barbara smiled. 'Not at all. He left not long after you did, actually. I'm sure he'll have had second thoughts about resigning today.'

'But last night it seemed that you were encouraging him to do just that! Barbs, if Grant leaves his job and goes off to London, I don't know what I'll do. I mean, he's never really said anything definite about us, and to tell the truth I haven't made up my mind about him either, but my job's getting really exciting and I don't want to give it up and follow him. I'd hate London, but if he went away I'd hate that too. I just don't know what to do.'

Andrea bit her thumbnail in frustration.

'Now listen to me.' Barbara leaned forward. 'In the first place, Grant is madly in love with you, I'm sure of that. You should have heard him singing your praises after you left last night. We hardly talked about anything else except you and your talent and general perfection! If he hasn't proposed yet, then I'm sure it's only because he's waiting for the right moment. I can tell he's the sort of man who needs to do things in style. And in the second place, if he should decide to move away, and you let a man like Grant slip through your fingers, you'll regret it for the rest of your life. So my advice to you is to practise saying 'yes' in the most gracious way you know how!'

'I suppose you're right,' said Andrea, even though she wasn't at all sure that

Barbara was. But she had the feeling that if she started discussing her doubts about Grant, then she wouldn't find a sympathetic ear.

The trouble with Grant, she thought crossly, is that he's just too darn smooth, and all the women he meets fall under his spell. Even Barbara.

★　★　★

During the weeks that followed, Andrea worked harder than she'd ever worked in her life. Luke had written a witty voice-over for the TV spot and she, Joe and Luke had stayed until nearly midnight choosing the actions to fit the words. The whole thing was then sent to a recording studio and when it came back, the Tweed brothers were invited into Joe's video studio for a preview.

'Charming, absolutely charming,' Arthur Tweed enthused as the video ended.

'Clever, really clever,' echoed his brother. 'I think I can guarantee that

141

United Northern will be most impressed.'

Along with the video, several newspaper advertisements were sent for United Northern's approval — all featuring the babies — and United Northern were ecstatic when they saw the campaign that Market Media had thought up for them. Their only regret was that the campaign would not appear for another two months.

'I wish we didn't have to wait for their last advertising campaign to come to an end.' Andrea sighed. 'I can't wait to see this on TV. And full-page advertisements in the national press — oh, boy!'

Luke smiled tolerantly. 'I envy you your excitement,' he said. 'Enjoy it, because it soon wears off. One of these days you'll be so used to seeing your work in the national papers that all you'll notice will be the mistakes you've made.'

'Mistakes? Did we make any?' She was horrified. Everything had looked perfect when the artwork was dispatched to the newspapers.

'Not that I could see. But when you

see your work in print there's always something you wish you'd done a little differently.'

'It's not exactly the first time I've see my work in print,' she said huffily. 'I was working here for ages before you came, remember?'

'How could I forget?' he said dryly. 'But let's face it, a full-page national advertisement will be a first for this studio.'

'I know,' she admitted. 'I just want to see it in print. Then I'll believe it.'

'Don't worry, it'll keep,' he assured her. 'In the meantime, we have other work to do!'

'Word has certainly got around that you're here,' she commented, looking at the worksheets piled up on his desk. 'Every one of them is from a new client. How on earth are we going to keep them all happy? Not that I'm complaining,' she said equably.

'Right, take this one for Supa-Vita-Gro, and see what you can come up with — the brief is inside the folder.

They manufacture vitamin drops and delicious stuff like garlic capsules and parsley pills. Go ahead and do your worst.' He caught her eye and grinned.

She noticed that he was wearing an old blue sweatshirt with two buttons missing, and marvelled at his complete lack of interest in his appearance. He usually came to work as though he were dressed for a weekend in the mountains and Andrea wondered again about the girl who shared his life — surely she could try to smarten him up just a little?

Then she pulled a face, remembering how much she herself hated Grant's efforts to get her to change, and reflected that this totally casual style was part of Luke's appeal and that she didn't really want him any different.

She settled down at her desk to think and doodle until inspiration struck.

When she and Jeannie took a break for lunch and were heading out of the studio on their way to the corner takeaway, Stephanie, the receptionist, was just putting down the phone.

'The big man is spending money like a drunken sailor,' she joked. 'First theatre tickets and now flowers — all in one day.'

Andrea frowned. 'Who do you mean?'

'Your boss! The hunk himself! First thing this morning he asked me to book two tickets for tonight for that musical that's on at the Imperial. Then just now he phoned and asked me to arrange delivery of flowers for some girl — let's see, here's the address, *Rosalind Kent, 15 Morningside Gardens.*' A bouquet and a corsage, if you please. I guess Miss Kent will be wearing the corsage when he takes her to the theatre.'

'Gosh, he must have a girlfriend after all,' Jeannie said. 'He's never mentioned anyone, has he, Andy? I wonder who she is?'

'He's probably got hundreds of girl-friends,' Andrea said sharply, her thoughts on what she'd just heard.

Morningside Gardens was a smart block, way over on the other side of town, yet when Luke had given Andrea a lift home he'd said that 'they' had taken a house just up the road from her own flat. That must mean he was taking out one girl while living with another! What a nerve!

Stop it, Andrea, she said to herself. Luke and his multiple love affairs have nothing to do with you.

'I wonder what she's like?' said Jeannie wistfully, while they waited at the takeaway for their toasted sandwiches to be made.

'Who?'

'Luke's girlfriend — Rosalind whatever-her-name-is. I bet she's beautiful. Don't you think he's divine, Andy? I love tall men. I bet he looks fantastic when he's all dressed up for the theatre.'

As hard as she tried, Andrea just couldn't picture Luke in smart or formal clothes. And that was a side of him that she was never likely to see, either; not while his idea of smart wear for the office consisted of a pair of clean jeans and a T-shirt.

I wonder if his live-in lady will iron his shirt for tonight, she thought, feeling sorry for the poor women, who was probably going to be told a lie about a business dinner. Some men are pretty awful to their girlfriends, she decided, but Luke takes the cake.

Just before six o'clock that evening, the phone rang. Andrea was about to leave for the day but she picked it up.

'Studio,' she said. 'Andrea speaking.'

'Is Luke Sullivan there at the moment?' It was a woman's voice, soft and musical.

'Sorry but he's already left,' she answered, wondering which of Luke's women this was.

'Oh, dear, I really wanted a word with him before tomorrow. You haven't his home number by any chance?'

'Sorry, I haven't, but you could leave a message and I'll see he gets it first thing in the morning?'

This obviously wasn't his date for the evening, and it couldn't be his live-in lady, either.

The whole town is full of his girlfriends, Andrea thought crossly, and I'm not his messenger service.

'Please ask him to phone Penelope as soon as he can,' said the voice on the line. 'It's really rather urgent.'

'If I see him, I'll be sure to tell him. Does he know your phone number?'

'Oh, yes. Tell him I must speak to him before he comes over tomorrow.'

Heavens! One tonight and another one tomorrow; he *was* keeping busy.

She wrote, '*Penelope called, please phone her, urgent*', and left the note propped up against his telephone.

Hailey, Rosalind and Penelope, she mused. I bet they all think they're the only ones in his life. Poor women, how little they know.

★   ★   ★

The phone was ringing as she opened the door to her flat. She dropped her shopping on the sofa and ran to answer it. It was Barbara.

'Hi there, are you too busy for a natter?'

Andrea looked at that morning's dishes lying reproachfully in the sink and at the basket of washing waiting to be taken to the launderette.

'Not at all,' she said. 'What's new with you?'

'That nice man of yours came to visit me again, that's what.' Barbara's voice bubbled happily. 'Did you ask him to?'

'Grant? Why, no. I hope he didn't bore you talking about his job again?'

'Absolutely not! I think he's a lovely man and I think you're a very lucky girl to have him,' said Barbara. 'He's got the most marvellous speaking voice, hasn't he? So deep and sincere, with such a lovely timbre. So masculine — although, of course, I suppose I'd notice his voice more than you would. I'm sure he's very handsome, too.'

'Yes, he is,' said Andrea, smiling.

'And he's very ambitious, isn't he? He really knows a lot about the world of advertising. I'm sure he'll go far. I

149

can see why you rave about him.'

Andrea felt a little pang of — was it jealousy? Don't be daft, she thought, this is Barbara. She needs as many people popping in to chat to her as she can get. It was very good of Grant to call on her again.

'What else did you talk about besides his work?'

'Oh, he talked about his mother, and his beautiful family home. He adores his mother, doesn't he? She must be quite a woman. I'd love to meet her. But I expect I will — at your wedding.'

'Wedding!' Andrea laughed. 'I don't know about a wedding, Barbs. I mean, there are a few problems — for one thing, he hasn't proposed. And then there's that mother of his. She's Super-woman! You should see the way she obsesses over the housework! And there was something about the way Grant concentrated on pleasing her. It made me feel — I don't know — left out, I suppose. He seemed to change com-pletely when he was at Applethorpe. He let his mother spoil him terribly and wait on him hand and foot — it was almost as if he became a little boy again.'

'Well, I suppose a mother likes to spoil her only son, no matter how old he is,' Barbara reasoned. 'Anyway, stop looking for faults in this scenario! Imagine having a place like Applethorpe just waiting for you to take over! All that luxury and space. You'll wonder how you ever lived in a cramped little flat with no garden. I remember my house; I did so enjoy my little rose garden before the accident . . . '

Barbara's voice trailed off into silence and Andrea could hear the tears near the surface.

'You haven't seen Applethorpe,' she interrupted briskly. 'It's enormous. And you didn't hear his mother going on about how she's keeping it beautiful for Grant's wife. Barbs, I'd have to polish that furniture for twenty-four hours day to keep it looking the way she does! She obviously doesn't regard me as wife material anyway, and I honestly can't see myself living in that high-gloss museum.'

'Well, perhaps Applethorpe wouldn't suit Grant either, at first,' Barbara conceded. 'He can hardly work in town and live so far out in the country, not if you're working too; it's just not practical.'

'Barbara, that's all very well, but the man hasn't produced a ring yet, so all this talk is a bit premature.'

'He will, he will. Trust your Auntie Barbara. I have a positive feeling about this romance! Anyway, when you see him again, tell him I enjoyed his visit. Next time, you must come too.'

'Hey, I work, remember? Grant can pop out of the office any time; he's always off seeing clients and he's got nobody keeping tabs on him.'

'Talking of keeping tabs, how's the terrible Luke?'

'He's fine. Though Casanova would be a better name for him. He seems to have hundreds of girlfriends around.'

'Well, you said he was good-looking.

Is he still bossing you about?'

'No so much. I think I'm getting that under control!'

They laughed, and Andrea rang off, promising to see her friend over the weekend.

The dirty dishes leered at her from the kitchen. OK, she grumbled, I'm coming.

★   ★   ★

One afternoon some days later, Luke walked slowly through the studio, his hands in his pockets, shaking the keys inside them irritably.

He looked at Andrea speculatively then crossed to her desk.

'Busy tonight?' he asked abruptly. As it happened, she knew Grant was once more entertaining business clients, and a long evening together with her ironing board awaited her.

'Why do you ask?'

'I've just had a call from Norris West; he's a director of United Northern.

They're having some sort of bash tonight and they'd like us to come.'

'Us?' she queried. 'They want you, they don't want me. They don't know me.'

'Us, meaning their advertising agents. So that's you and me, kiddo.'

'What about Tweedledum and Tweedle-dee?'

'Normally they'd be there like a shot, but one of them is in London and the other one is home in bed with bronchitis.'

She stared at him dubiously. 'I don't know. I mean, what would I do at a party like that? I wouldn't know anyone to talk to. And I'm not dressed for it.'

He grinned. 'You'll do what people always do at these awful parties; you'll eat and drink all the soggy little bits and pieces they provide so you won't have to make supper when you get home. And you'll know me, so if the rest of them are too boring, then you and I can always talk.'

She had to admit that the idea of going out with Luke and seeing him in a social setting instead of in the studio was attractive. And it was on business anyway, she reasoned — like when Grant goes out with his clients.

'It doesn't start until seven o'clock so you've plenty of time to go home and change,' he told her. 'In fact, I could give you a lift to your flat and then pick you up on my way back. As you may have noticed, I'm not exactly dressed in my party best either.'

'If these sort of parties are so awful, why do you want to go at all?' she hedged.

'I don't, but life isn't all just a mad round of pleasure,' he said. 'Come on, it's part of your job as my assistant to help me out with this sort of thing.'

'But you don't have to take me, so why don't you take — ' she hesitated ' — someone else?'

She'd been about to say, 'Rosalind, Hailey or Penelope,' but thought better of it.

'Because it's you I want to take,' he said firmly. 'OK?'

'OK,' she agreed faintly.

An Evening with Luke

On the dot of seven o'clock there was a knock on Andrea's door. When she opened it, she gave an involuntary gasp at the sight of her art director, now magnificently clad in a black dinner jacket, its perfect cut accentuating his wide shoulders. And in his hand he held a delicate corsage of rosebuds and ferns.

'Gosh, I hardly recognised you!' she blurted. 'You're all dressed up!'

'The things I do for my job are incredibly demanding,' he answered with a straight face. 'But when duty calls, I answer.'

'I see you scrub up not too badly yourself, Miss Ross. Not badly at all.'

He leaned forward and pinned the corsage to her dress.

She looked down, avoiding his eyes, aware of his warm, male smell and the surprising gentleness of his touch. He

157

gives roses to all the girls he takes out, she reminded herself.

'Yes, well, I know you prefer me in sensible clothes and flat shoes, but this was all I could find in the rush,' she muttered, blushing as she felt his gaze travel approvingly over her.

She was thankful she'd decided to make an effort for this evening and knew she looked her best in her blue velvet mini-dress.

He gave her silk-encased legs in their high heels a long look.

'You'll definitely do,' he said. 'I can see I'm going to have to stand between you and the crowds of admirers. I'll probably finish up bruised and battered while defending your honour.'

'That should be fun,' she said lightly. 'I'd quite like to see you getting punched on the nose!'

* * *

When they reached the party, Luke excused himself for a moment while he went to look for Norris West.

Not knowing what to do with her hands, Andrea accepted a glass of wine from a passing waiter and started nibbling at a nearby plate of snacks.

The plush boardroom of United Northern was filled with a noisy crowd and she wondered how soon they could decently leave. Her head was starting to ache already and she realised she was very hungry. She'd missed lunch and in the rush to wash her hair and get ready for this party, she'd had no time to make even a sandwich. The soggy canapes which Luke had predicted and the smell of cigarette smoke did nothing to ease her hunger or her headache and she wished she'd never agreed to come.

A hand on her shoulder startled her and she swung round in relief to see Luke standing next to her with an elderly man in tow.

'Andrea, I'd like you to meet our host, Mr Norris West.'

Norris West smiled at her in open

admiration. 'Luke's assistant! My, my, what a lucky man,' he said, grasping her hand and holding it for slightly too long. 'I want to tell you, my dear, we all think the new advertising campaign is very good, very good indeed.'

'Thank you,' she said, at a loss for words.

'It's like a breath of fresh air. Something quite different. Our decision to change to Market Media was an excellent one and I can see input from the — ah — younger generation is going to be a great improvement. We have to move with the times.'

'Er, yes, you do,' she answered. Darn it, why didn't Luke help her out and say something, instead of grinning at her discomfort? I'm no good at these conversations, she thought wretchedly.

'I look forward to working with you both for a long time to come,' Norris West continued, still holding on to her hand. 'And, Luke — you must be sure to bring the charming Andrea with you next time you visit our offices. Can't

keep a beauty like this all to yourself!'
He gave her hand a parting squeeze and
went off to join another group of
guests.

'Old goat,' Luke murmured as their
host was absorbed back into the crowd.
'Sorry about that.'

'I didn't mind him too much,' she
said, laughing. 'It's nice to be appreciated sometimes!'

'Unappreciated, are you?' he asked
speculatively. 'What's the matter with
lover boy?'

'You mean Grant? Nothing at all,' she
returned tartly.

He pulled a face. 'You didn't mean
me, I hope? Have I been lacking in
appreciation of my assistant?'

'I didn't mean anyone. It was just a
remark — oh, heavens, no!'

Before she could stop him, he'd
taken a handful of flowers from an
arrangement on a low table nearby and
handed them to her with a flourish,
bowing low and taking her hand in his.

'Mademoiselle is too, too ravishing,'

he murmured, kissing her palm and then covering the inside of her arm with little kisses. People around them turned and smiled.

'Luke's at it again,' said a woman's voice indulgently.

Andrea clutched the dripping flowers and glared at the top of his head, still bent over her hand.

'Luke! Stop it! Please!' she gasped with embarrassment. 'What on earth do you think you're doing?'

'I am practising my appreciation of you,' he said wickedly. 'It's easier than I thought. I could even get to like it.'

'If you don't stop right now I am walking straight out of here,' she hissed.

'OK,' he said cheerfully, dropping her hand immediately. 'I'm very sorry to have embarrassed you, but I thought women liked receiving flowers.'

'Why must you act like such an idiot?' she said furiously. 'Everyone's looking at us. I'm never going anywhere with you ever again.'

Just then they were joined by a man

162

who smiled broadly at Luke and then spoke to him in a drawling American accent. 'Sullivan, isn't it? Remember me? Dusty's Bar and Grill on Broadway, last Christmas? You were with that fabulous blonde graphic artist called — wait, yes — Hailey, and I was with that rather bad tempered lady who has recently become — I'm happy to say — my ex-wife.'

'Of course I remember you,' Luke answered with a welcoming grin. 'Mike, isn't it? And you were marketing computers, weren't you?'

'Right. I heard you'd come back over here. Bring Hailey with you?'

Luke stood perfectly still, his hands tensing around his glass.

'No,' he answered shortly. 'I came back from the States alone.'

'Oh, now I remember. She was involved in an accident somewhere on a mountain, wasn't she?' the American continued. 'When they had that freak snowstorm that winter? What a shame. What a waste. Lovely girl. The man

163

who took her up there at that time of year must have been crazy.'

Luke's face had turned ashen and Andrea noticed his jaw stiffen, and a little muscle twitching in his temple. Suddenly she knew whose accident it had been that had put him off serious rock climbing for ever.

'So, Mike, what are you doing over here?' Luke forced out the words with an effort. 'Business or pleasure?'

Mike had noticed nothing of the reaction his words had caused and answered easily. Soon they were deep in the sort of 'do you remember' conversation that excludes anyone who wasn't there at the time.

'Well, and who's this? Aren't you going to introduce us?' The American broke off suddenly and leaned towards Andrea, offering his hand.

'I know it's not just that Luke has no manners at all,' he continued, 'but unless he's asked, he'll never introduce anyone as lovely as you. I'm Mike Cooper — and you are?'

'This is Andy,' said Luke. 'My assistant. And she's not looking for a boyfriend, so take that hopeful little gleam out of your eye!'

The way he said it made it sound as though she was his exclusive property, thought Andrea indignantly.

'I'm Andrea Ross,' she said pleasantly. 'Luke and I have been working on the new campaign for United Northern.'

'Aha,' he said. 'Trust Luke to find himself a gorgeous assistant.'

'He didn't find me, he inherited me with the studio,' she answered, determined not to appear like another of the seemingly endless supply of women that Luke appeared to have at his beck and call.

'What a nice legacy.' Mike grinned, giving her a teasing look. 'Tell me, what's he like to work for? Does he still shout at everyone and order them about? I have to say, he had a terrible reputation in New York!'

'Actually,' she answered, 'he's quite

all right if you know how to handle him. I just make sure he's fed and watered regularly.'

Luke stared at her in amazement while Mike exploded in laughter.

'She's got your number, Luke! I think you've met your match here, old man!'

She glanced at Luke and was slightly alarmed by the narrow look in his eye.

'Watch out, I bite if I'm not treated properly!' he growled softly.

'I didn't mean it — I was only teasing!' she protested, half laughing.

'I'm not,' he said, putting his hand on her shoulder.

Andrea felt a sudden shock at the contact. His hand was hard and warm and her traitorous body reacted to his touch. She felt herself starting to tremble but Luke seemed oblivious to her reaction.

Without releasing his grasp, he turned back to his American acquaintance.

'Time we were leaving, Mike. Nice to see you. I'll give you a ring next week.'

'Right, let's get together for lunch.

Goodbye, Andrea, lovely to meet you.'

Luke propelled her down the stairs to his van.

What now, she wondered. Is he going to suggest coffee for two at my place? How do I handle this? How do I want to handle it?

But his next words surprised her.

'Hungry? Feel like a good square meal?'

'Oh, yes,' she admitted. 'I could eat a horse.'

'The place I have in mind doesn't have horse on the menu, but do you like Chinese food?'

'Love it!' she said.

'Good. Me too. Next stop, China-town.' He swung the van towards the city centre. 'I warned you those sorts of parties are horrible,' he continued, 'everyone talks a lot of nonsense and there's too much noise and never any proper food.'

'Oh, really? I thought the conversation was charming,' she said airily.

'Yes, well, every single male there has

joined the Andy Ross fan club, that's for sure,' he grumbled. 'I told you I'd be beating them off with a stick.'

'You sound cross. Was it so difficult?' She realised with a small shock that she was flirting with him.

He looked at her quizzically but said nothing until they drew up outside the Green Dragon restaurant.

★　★　★

Tucked away behind a palm tree at a small table for two, a bottle of cold white wine and the remains of supper between them, Andrea leaned back and smiled contentedly at Luke. They'd slowly worked their way through bowls of sweet and sour pork, and spicy chicken wings, talking almost without pause.

They'd begun by discussing art, gone on to music, politics, fox hunting, chocolate cake, making bread, the psychology of training animals — how ever did we get on to that, she wondered in amazement.

168

'Feeling better?'

'Yes, much.' She sighed happily. 'It's funny how you always start off thinking you can eat everything on the menu but with Chinese food you never can. It's delicious though.'

'Save a little space for the cookies,' he said.

A companionable silence hung between them while they waited for the green tea that he'd ordered, and she felt completely relaxed.

'I hope you didn't think I was being rude at the party,' she said suddenly. 'I mean, saying you had to be fed and so on. I just resented the way your friend talked to me.'

'Good heavens, no. It just made me remember how hungry I was.'

He crossed his arms and looked at her intently, his grey eyes serious.

'So, I'm OK to work for, am I? Would you say you're happy with the changes I've made?'

'Of course,' she answered without hesitation. 'Although we'd heard — I

169

mean, Jeannie and I were both pretty terrified before you came. You did come with an awful reputation!'

'That was then. This is now.' He looked almost embarrassed. 'I know I used to have a bad name for being impossible to work with. Believe me, enough people have told me so! But the problem was, I went too far, too fast. I was your typical whizz kid. Horrible!'

She laughed. 'You don't seem like a whizz kid. I've always thought that a whizz kid was someone of about eighteen who was terribly clever.'

'Whereas I'm positively elderly and not very bright?' he finished.

'Oh, no,' she protested. 'You're bright, all right; in fact, I think you're just fishing for compliments.'

'Could I have a deep-seated insecurity problem?' he asked hopefully.

'That I doubt.'

'It's a fact though,' he mused. 'I had so much luck when I started out, it was unbelievable. I was running an advertising studio by the time I was twenty-two.

The advertising accounts that fell into my lap were fantastic and there seemed to be a sort of snowball effect — when people knew I was handling one huge account they'd ask me to handle theirs as well. In the end I was flying over to America for a meeting and back again the next day, touching base and then flying to Paris for a working dinner. No wonder I was impossible!'

'What made you go to work in New York then?' she asked curiously. 'Wasn't it even harder over there?'

'I liked the buzz of working in the States. The pace was terrific and there's something about New York that got to me. And the people are marvellous. It was an advertising man's heaven. But then something happened.'

He paused and cleared his throat. 'I guess I suddenly just got tired of the party scene. I sat back and realised that I was missing out on a normal life.'

'And you missed having mountains on your doorstep?'

'Well, no. America's not exactly short

of mountains. But coming back was something I was ready to do.'

'You're so lucky,' she said wistfully. 'You've done your travelling and you seem happy to settle. I'd give anything to travel overseas — anywhere!'

As she said it, she realised it was true. While she was at college, she'd always planned to travel. To hitchhike across the States or Canada, to backpack across Australia, or to take a bus through India. But once she'd met Grant, all her thoughts of adventure had gone. Now, listening to Luke, she felt a sudden urge to pack her rucksack and go somewhere far away. But even as she thought about it, she knew Grant would never want to go with her.

'What's stopping you then?' he queried. 'Everyone should get out and see the world, especially you. Lymchester's a nice place to live but it's not the most exciting place on earth! You should go now, while you've nothing to keep you here. Or have you? Something to keep you here, I mean. You're not serious about that fellow Grant?' His bantering tone made it sound ridiculous to admit that she was.

'I think I might be,' she said slowly. 'In fact I'm pretty sure I am.'

'That means you're not,' he said decisively. 'Nobody thinks they're in love. They know it. And everyone else knows it, too. If you were in love with Grant you wouldn't look so depressed and anxious every time you talk about him.'

'I do not!' she cried. 'And you're hardly an expert on how I feel.'

'Maybe not, but I know how you should feel,' he said firmly.

'You're one to talk!' She was stung. 'You've got half the women in this town thinking you're in love with them!'

'Is that so?' Luke raised his eyebrows in amusement. 'But I'm not. If I was, they'd know it, not just think it. Now, how about some green tea?'

He handed her one of the fortune cookies that had arrived with the tea and she broke it in half, unrolling the little piece of paper from inside.

'What does it say?'

''Go slowly with man in fast car',' she read, flushing.

'You see. You can't argue with the wisdom of the East!' he said triumphantly. 'Come on, it's time for me to take you home.'

With a start she saw they were the last people in the restaurant, and she left the table regretfully.

When they reached her flat, she tensed herself for his next move, unconsciously moving over towards the passenger door.

'Relax, little Miss Ross,' he said, 'the big bad wolf isn't going to eat you.'

'I know that,' she said with dignity.

I'm not going to invite him in for coffee, I'm not, she thought. I'm letting myself get far too close to this man as it is.

'I'm not even going to invite myself up for coffee,' he added kindly.

'I wasn't going to ask you anyway,' she said crossly.

Then he kissed her lightly on her cheek.

'Thanks for helping me out this evening.'

'Oh — that was all right. I enjoyed myself,' she answered lamely.

'So did I. Good night, Andrea.'

Watching him drive away, she felt strangely deflated.

★   ★   ★

The next day she'd planned to see a film with Jeannie and Stephanie after work, but a phone call from Grant just as they were about to leave forced her to change her mind.

'I need to see you. I've got something to tell you,' he said mysteriously.

About an hour later, he arrived at her flat and announced triumphantly, 'As of today, I am a free man.' He strode around the room looking extremely pleased with himself. 'No more of that old fool Forbes making my life a misery and talking to me as if I'm some kind of office boy.'

'W-what do you mean? You haven't really resigned from Mattler Horne?'

'Yes. It was high time I left that bunch of fuddy-duddies. They were holding me back. Every idea I had, they put some obstacle in my way. Their ideas were much too conservative.'

'But what will you do now?' She dreaded his reply, but to her surprise he made no mention of leaving for London.

'Oh, I've plenty of irons in the fire — something will come up. I've got one big advantage: I'll be taking Fastabank with me. They're my clients now, and they'll stick with me wherever I go. So any agency will snap me up when I bring a client that size with me. They have a really huge advertising budget.'

'Fastabank?' she queried. 'You've never mentioned before that they'd given you their advertising account. I remember your mother mentioning something about them, when I was staying that weekend — '

'Yes, well, you'll remember that the

chairman of Fastabank happens to be a cousin of Mother's. He gave me their advertising account to handle a couple of months ago. That made Mattler Horne sit up and take notice of me, all right! They'll regret — I mean, they'll miss that big account in future. So I'm not worried about finding another position as accounts executive. This time I'm going for a senior post and I'm going to be pretty choosy. So tonight, we celebrate! What do you say to dinner and a spot of dancing at Michel's?'

'Isn't that very expensive?' she said dubiously. 'Shouldn't you be saving money, now you haven't got a job? We could always just have a pizza somewhere.'

'Andy, don't fuss. And stop looking so gloomy! This is the best thing I've done in a long time. You don't want me to be stuck as a junior account executive all my life, do you? And that's just what I would be if I stayed on.'

'But I thought you enjoyed your work?'

'Well, I've enjoyed some of it, but I'm

aiming to run my own show one of these days. I've no intention of working for someone else for very long.'

He sat down on the sofa and frowned.

'This sofa cover should be thrown away,' he said pettishly. 'It's looking very tatty. It's not as if you're some impoverished student, Andrea. Why don't you smarten this place up a bit?'

'But I love this throw,' she protested. 'I bought it on the market from an Indian lady. It's woven with pure silk. I know it's a bit old but I think it's beautiful. The colours are so subtle.'

'It's very old and full of holes,' he said, getting up abruptly. 'I wish you'd get rid of it. And while you're about it, it's time you bought some decent chairs to sit on. What would you do if Mother came to call? You could hardly expect her to sit on this.'

'Your mother? But she's not planning to visit me, surely?' she asked in alarm.

'Not as far as I know, but she might take it into her head to pop in next time she's in town to get to know you better,' said Grant. 'Anyway, hurry up and put on something nice. We're going out. I feel like dancing.'

At least he's not planning to leave Lymchester, she thought, looking at her reflection in the bathroom mirror as she quickly applied some lipstick.

And most people who met Grant liked him at once, so he should have no trouble finding a better position.

Andrea relaxed and began to look forward to the evening ahead, which turned out to be one of the best evenings they'd ever enjoyed together.

Michel's was a discreet little restaurant with a small dance floor and a band that played the sort of music meant for people who wanted to hold each other close.

'You're looking particularly gorgeous tonight, sweetie,' he whispered as she shut her eyes and laid her head on his shoulder as they swayed together to the music.

During their meal of fillet mignon

and a bottle of champagne, which he'd ordered despite her protests about the price, he entertained her with stories about Mattler Horne and the people there. He'd never spoken to her about any of them them before, but now it seemed that, now he'd left them, he felt he could tell her about all sorts of funny incidents.

Andrea couldn't help noticing that he didn't seem to have liked any of his former colleagues very much. Well, she'd always known he didn't get on with Mr Forbes, but the way he described them, everyone there had been either lazy, inefficient or down-right dishonest. According to Grant, he'd spent a lot of his time covering up other people's faults without any gratitude from those he'd helped.

'You're well out of it,' she declared, after hearing about a secretary who had left some irreplaceable documents in a taxi and how he'd chased all over town to retrieve them for her without so much as a thank you.

'You're right. Anyway, I've decided to give old Harringer of Darcy Jones a ring on Monday. Let them know I'm available. I don't see myself being at a loose end for long.'

'I'm sure they'll offer you something,' she said loyally.

'And I won't accept any less than half as much salary again as I was getting at Mattler Horne.'

'Now you're talking!' she joked, putting her nose into her glass and enjoying the tickles from the bubbles. Privately she hoped Grant would accept whatever they offered him and not quibble about the salary. If he had to be without work for any length of time he'd be so depressed that he'd probably leave for London. And then what would she do?

'I mean it. It's time I was earning some real money. We're going to need it.'

'We?' she queried, swallowing her mouthful of steak. Here it comes, she thought. A proper proposal. Barbara had been right! He was just waiting for the right time and place.

'Me and Mummy, of course.' Then he saw the look on her face and added, 'You didn't think . . . Oh! You did!'

He grinned confidently at her, his eyes twinkling above his champagne glass.

'I don't think this is either the time or the place for that sort of thing, sweetie!'

She smiled down at her plate and said nothing.

Oh, Grant, she thought, you're hopeless. But I do love you. I think.

A Breath of Fresh Air

The following day was Saturday. Andrea forced herself out of bed half an hour earlier than usual, donned her shorts and training shoes, and set off across the park for a good run. The early morning air was clear and crisp and in no time the cobwebs from her late night had blown away. Alone on the quiet paths beneath the trees except for an occasional squirrel, she increased her pace for the sheer enjoyment of speed.

Usually, when she reached the gate at the other side of the park, she turned back. But she felt so good that morning that she decided to carry on a bit longer. As she pounded along the pavement, puffing slightly, she saw a familiar van parked outside an old house. She slowed to a walk, wondering if she'd see Luke or his girlfriend in the garden.

A soft whine caught her attention.

Sitting behind the gate was the biggest dog Andrea had ever seen. It stood up on its hind legs, tail wagging joyfully, its huge brown eyes almost level with her own.

'Hello there,' she said softly, rubbing its shaggy grey coat. 'What's your name then?'

The dog tried to lick her face, ecstatic with this attention.

'OK, Jessie, that's enough. Down, girl,' commanded a deep, familiar voice and Luke appeared from around the corner of the house. He smiled in welcome when he saw Andrea. 'You're out early! How did you find us?'

'I wasn't looking for you! I was just out for a run and — '

'Well, you look as though you could do with a rest. Take a break and come in for a cup of coffee.'

She hesitated, but her curiosity got the better of her and she accepted gratefully.

He opened the gate to let her in, holding back the huge dog with one hand.

'Don't pay any attention to Jessie. She's so friendly that she can be a bit of a pest sometimes, especially if she spots you're a dog lover!'

'She's right, I am. What breed is she?'

'Irish wolfhound. She got papers that prove she's practically Irish royalty, but luckily she doesn't know that, so we get along fine.'

Luke led Andrea into a big kitchen, in the centre of which was a huge scrubbed table, and he pulled out a chair for her.

'Sit there,' he commanded. 'This will only take a minute. How about some toast with our coffee? I was just about to make some.'

'Lovely,' she said, suddenly starving.

Jessie lay stretched across the floor under the table, her huge head resting lightly on Andrea's foot, and her eyes watching Luke as he made the toast, filled glasses with fruit juice, and placed marmalade and butter on the table.

Andrea leaned back lazily and looked around the spacious kitchen. The room felt somehow familiar and it struck her suddenly that it was very like her mother's kitchen in Scotland, with pots of herbs on the windowsill and a big pine kitchen dresser across one wall.

'The dresser came from my folk's home,' he said, noticing her interest. 'When I was a kid I spent my happiest times in my mother's kitchen and when they sold up their house, I just couldn't let someone else buy that dresser. I've had it in storage for nearly ten years and when we came here I had to find a kitchen big enough for it. Crazy, hey?'

'No, not crazy. I think that's nice. It's a great piece of furniture; my mother has one just like it. What's in this big dish?'

She pointed to a cloth-covered bowl in the centre of the table.

He moved it out of the way, on to the dresser. 'Bread. I make my own whenever I have time. Nothing beats homemade brown bread.'

'Really?' She was delighted. 'I thought I recognised the smell. Is it still rising?

My mum wraps hers in an old blanket and puts it near the Aga to rise.'

'Yep. This will be ready to bake this evening. If you're really good, I'll bring you some to taste on Monday.'

She shook her head in amusement. 'I've never heard of a man baking bread!'

'I must remind you, young lady, that all the best chefs are men and so it naturally follows that all the best bakers are men, too.'

'I know you think I'm going to argue that point, but I'll wait until I've tasted your efforts! You'll have to be pretty darn good to beat my mum's whole-wheat bread.'

'That's not fair. I bet you scoff your mum's bread while it's still hot from the oven. Nothing beats hot bread! But I'll accept the challenge.'

She kept listening for footsteps and expected the kitchen door to open at any minute. Surely Luke's girlfriend would hear him talking to someone and come through?

Unless she was the type to sleep late? Maybe he was planning to take her breakfast in bed? But no, he'd only put out two cups.

'I haven't seen you running this way before,' he remarked.

'I usually just run around the park, but today I felt like keeping going,' she said, admiring the efficient way he prepared breakfast. He certainly knew his way around his kitchen, probably because the sleeping girlfriend was far too gorgeous to do anything as mundane as make food.

Soon the smell of freshly-ground coffee filled the room and Andrea sniffed appreciatively.

'Mmm, delicious,' she said. 'This sure beats the coffee at work!'

'Anything beats the coffee at work.' He grinned, placing hot crisp toast and a pot of marmalade between them. They ate in companionable silence for a few minutes until he asked, 'So what are your plans for the rest of the day?'

'Oh, cleaning my flat, I suppose.

Shopping — that sort of thing.'

He smiled. 'In other words, nothing that can't wait. I've got a much better idea.'

'And that is?'

'Come with us for walk up Mount Ayliff. It's not far. Half an hour's drive and then it's only a three-hour walk to the summit.'

She considered his invitation.

She hadn't had a really good day out on the hills since she'd left college.

Grant, of course, would probably be furious if she told him she'd spent the day climbing with Luke but, as usual, he hadn't made any definite arrangement for the two of them to meet up that day.

And it wasn't as if she and Luke would be alone — the 'us' sounded as though the girlfriend would be going along with them. His eyes held hers expectantly.

'I'd love to,' she heard herself say.

'Great! Jessie needs a bit of exercise, don't you, girl?'

The feathery tail beat a tattoo on the floor.

'You'll want to change,' he added briskly. 'I'll run you back to your flat. Have you got some decent walking shoes? And you'll need a sweater.'

'Yes, boss,' she said meekly.

'Right then.'

He left the room and returned a minute later carrying a cagoule and a small backpack.

'Let's go!'

'But what about . . . isn't anyone else coming?'

'Just Jessie.'

⋆ ⋆ ⋆

Sitting against a rock at the top of Mount Ayliff, Andrea ran her hand through Jessie's rough coat and marvelled at the view. A patchwork of farmlands stretched in all directions and, in the distance, the city of Lymchester appeared like a smudge of smog on the horizon. High above, a pair of hawks wheeled and swooped and the only sound to break the silence was the wind in the grass.

'It's lovely to be out of town, isn't it?' she said dreamily, closing her eyes and leaning back against the rock.

The sun warmed her whole body and Andrea felt herself relaxing and drifting off in a haze of contentment. She could have been back home in Scotland on the hills above Lannock with her sister.

She remembered how the two of them used to escape up into the hills after school, and lie on the grass, making plans for the day they would leave the village and start living their real lives.

Travelling the world together had been one of their big plans, but in the end only Annabelle flew away, having married an Australian guy almost as soon as she'd left college.

After that, Andrea had started work and had somehow shelved her own dreams of far-away places.

Something tickled her cheek and she

brushed it away without opening her eyes. When it tickled again a second time, she waved her hand and opened her eyes to see Luke leaning over her, stroking her face with grass stalk.

His eyes were very close to hers and there was a small smile playing around his lips. 'Wake up, sleepy head,' he said huskily.

She lay where she was, gazing up at him, and he stared into her eyes for what seemed like eternity. She was almost overwhelmed by the desire to be kissed by him and to feel his strong brown arms around her.

She swallowed and was unable to look away, sure that he could hear the thudding of her heart. It was as though a magnet was drawing him closer and closer to her and, powerless to stop whatever was going to happen, her hands lifted to his shoulders to pull him towards her.

But suddenly he pushed himself away and sat up without a word, breaking the spell. Then he sat gazing fixedly out across the valley, his breath rasping.

She pushed herself up on to her elbows, her heart pounding. Waves of conflicting emotions washed over her — regret that he hadn't kissed her being the strongest of them. But she was also angry with herself for responding to him as she had.

'I wasn't asleep,' she said in a small voice.

'I was just checking,' he said roughly. 'We'll have to start back soon.'

Didn't something almost happen a minute ago, she wondered, her mind numb. Or was I the only one who noticed it? Well, if that's the way he's going to play it . . .

'Oh, must we go? This is so lovely,' she said lightly. 'It's quite the best Saturday morning I've had in ages.'

'What do you usually do with your Saturdays? Spend them with Grant?' He turned back to face her, his voice level, with no trace of the emotion of a minute before.

'Well, yes. We go to the shops, or to

see a film. Sometimes we just watch television.' She trailed off, realising that this sounded a bit dull, and felt, obscurely, that she was being disloyal to Grant. 'We enjoy it,' she added.

'Grant's not exactly Action Man, is he?' he said. 'He doesn't sound like a very good choice for someone like you.'

Taken aback, she stammered, 'But you're so wrong! You know nothing about him — he's hardworking and clever, and . . . '

'And kind to animals and good to his mother, of course,' Luke finished with an edge of sarcasm. 'I'm sure he's a saint. But he's not the man for you. And you're wrong when you say I know nothing about him. Don't forget the advertising world is a small place — I happen to know quite a lot about your Mr Carter and I heard yesterday that he lost his job at Mattler Horne in rather nasty circumstances.'

'That's not true! He didn't lose his job — he resigned. Other people were always taking the credit for what he did and he was getting nowhere because of it.'

He looked at her quizzically.

'That's not what I heard.'

'I don't want to know what you heard! I'm telling you what happened! And how can you listen to gossip and repeat it without knowing the facts?'

'Which are?'

'The facts are that the senior partner at Mattler Horne was always finding fault with him and quashing his ideas, and the last straw was when he started shouting at Grant in front of all the staff. How do you think he felt? He had to resign; he couldn't let himself be spoken to like that!'

'Mmm. Well, it's no business of mine.'

'You're right, it's not,' she said savagely, standing up. 'I think we'd better go back now.'

She picked up her windcheater, quivering with fury. How dare he talk about Grant in this way, spreading malicious rumours when he knew nothing about the matter?

All she wanted to do was get off the mountain and drive home as quickly as possible.

The beauty of their surroundings had lost its charm and she hurried ahead, putting as much distance between herself and Luke as she possibly could.

Her mind seethed as she half walked, half ran down the mountain path. Could there be any truth in what he'd said? What did 'nasty circumstances' mean? Or was this some twisted way of showing he was jealous, making insinuations about his rival? But did he really see Grant as a rival? She couldn't blind herself to the way he'd looked at her during the past few weeks, nor the hot current of attraction that she, in turn, felt for him.

Luke kept pace with her, walking behind her in silence, but Jessie walked alongside her, pushing her head under her hand every now and then, demanding to know what was wrong.

'Andy, listen. If I spoke out of turn

then I'm sorry,' said Luke finally, his voice gruff. 'You're right. It's none of my business.'

'Just leave the subject of Grant alone,' she snapped. 'My private life has nothing to do with you.'

'You're such an honest, naive girl, I just don't want to see you get hurt.'

'You just can't resist telling me how to run my life, can you?' she flashed back at him. 'You're just so used to having everyone around you jump when you say jump. Well, for your information, he's not about to hurt me; in fact, he's about to make me very happy. Grant and I are going to be married. Now — I don't want to discuss it any more.'

They walked on in silence.

Travelling back to town, they exchanged polite remarks across a gulf which seemed to grow wider with every mile.

What possessed me to say I was going to marry Grant, she thought wretchedly. He hasn't even asked me. But he will. And when he does I'll say yes.

Luke halted the camper van outside her flat.

'Andy, I — '

'Thanks for the walk,' she said brightly, jumping out and slamming the door. 'See you on Monday.'

'Andy!' He leapt out and strode purposefully around to her gate, grabbing her arm to prevent her running up the steps. 'You can't leave like this. We've got to straighten things out. I've said I'm sorry, what more do you want?'

'Nothing,' she said. 'Really, nothing. It doesn't bother me. You just repeated something that isn't true. You've apologised. It's over.'

'It's not over. Are you really going to marry Grant or did you just say that to make me angry?'

'Why should it make you angry?' she parried coldly. 'I've been going out with Grant for months, what's so unusual about wanting to marry him?'

'Because he's wrong for you!' he growled. 'Heavens, woman, can't you see that? You won't have any sort of a life if you marry that — that tailor's dummy!'

'That's a typical Luke Sullivan comment!' she flung at him. 'Insulting him because he dresses well. Just because he doesn't go haring up mountains like you do, that makes him wrong for me? There's something a bit odd about your logic!'

'I told you, there's more to life than just settling down and having babies with that — that — with Grant,' he ended lamely.

'This is my life we're talking about!' she cried. 'I'll live it how I want to! Now let go of my arm and leave me alone!' She wrenched herself out of his grasp and ran up the stairs two at a time, fumbled with her key in the lock and fell on the sofa, sobbing.

★ ★ ★

Alone in her flat, Andrea relived that moment on top of the mountain. Waves of rage and remorse washing over her. How could she have been so fickle? She'd been prepared to forget about Grant and give herself up to the tidal wave of sensations that seemed to sweep through her whole body. It was lucky, really, that Luke had managed to so completely break the spell by talking such awful nonsense about the man to whom she was almost engaged. And yet, asked a small voice inside her, could there be any truth in what he'd said? Surely Grant would never lie to her?

To stop herself thinking about it, she opened a magazine and tried to read, but the words made no sense as the scene with Luke kept coming back to her. She knew she had never felt so passionately about any man as she had for that brief moment earlier, and remembering her lack of control she was frightened. It would be better if she stayed well out of the way of Luke Sullivan, she thought. Better for everyone.

When Grant called for her that evening, she opened the door and flew into his arms as if they'd been separated for a month instead of only one day.

She was careful to let nothing show on her face of the torment she'd been through during the afternoon and had repaired the ravages that a storm of crying had left on her face.

They stood in the open doorway, locked in an embrace.

'This is some hello!' Grant murmured approvingly, his kisses becoming more urgent.

She drew back, gasping, and smiled at him.

The familiar presence of Grant in her flat made sense of everything and put the whole day into its proper perspective.

This was the man she loved, and what had happened on Mount Ayliff had been a bad dream. She felt horribly guilty for even imagining herself being kissed and held by Luke. I must have been mad, she thought, as she snuggled against Grant.

'Mmm, I'm just so glad to see you.'

'So I see. I just hope all your visitors don't get a welcome like this!' he joked.

'No, only you.'

'That's good. Now, much as I'd like to continue this welcome party, could we resume it a bit later? I've managed to get tickets for that jazz concert and they're not going to hold the curtain for us. Let's go!'

She tucked her arm in his, and together they ran down the stairs.

I'm not going to say one word about his resignation from Mattler Horne, she decided.

★ ★ ★

On Monday, she walked into the studio with her head held high. She was determined not to give Luke the satisfaction of seeing her embarrassment. But she needn't have worried; he was out for the morning, and when he returned just before lunch, he gave Andrea only a brief glance.

'Not aching from the climb?' he asked her casually.

'Not at all, thanks,' she said coolly and bent her head over her work.

'What climb?' asked Jeannie as he went into his office.

'Oh — nothing. He and I just happened to meet when we were both out walking on the mountain,' she answered, flustered.

But if she'd hoped this answer would satisfy Jeannie, she was wrong.

'Which mountain? Who was he with? Was it that blonde girl in the photo?'

Andrea felt herself redden. Now why did I say that, she thought crossly, knowing she was hopeless at fibbing.

'Oh, it was Mount Ayliff. He was with some girl. I didn't notice her.'

'Didn't notice her!' squealed the younger girl. 'How could you not notice her? You'd surely have recognised the one in the photo that was on his desk that day. Do you think it could have been Rosalind, that girl he sent flowers to? How old was she?'

'Considerably older than you,' snapped Andrea. 'Luke's not a cradle snatcher, whatever his other faults.'

Jeannie stared at her in surprise. 'Don't be so snappy,' she said. 'You must have got out of the wrong side of bed this morning. I only asked.'

'Yes, well, never mind about Luke's social life, try to finish those layouts before lunch.'

Jeannie sniffed and turned her head away. Oh dear, thought Andrea, why did I have to snarl at her like that? I know she's got a crush on Luke. Why didn't I think faster and say he was with a male friend?

At lunchtime she tried to smooth things over by offering to buy Jeannie a toasted sandwich but the younger girl refused and went to lunch with Stephanie instead.

So Andrea was sitting alone at her desk when Luke came out of his office.

'Take a break,' he told her. 'There's no big rush on that job.'

'I'd rather get on with it, thanks,' she said.

'Come on, the sun's shining. Do you good to get out a bit.'

'No, really, I'm quite happy here,' she insisted, not meeting his eyes.

'Andrea, stop sulking!' he said severely. 'I apologised once, and that's all the apology you're going to get. Now, we've got to work together so you may as well make the best of it. You can start by taking that gloomy expression off your face.'

She gritted her teeth and stared at her computer screen, the lettering swimming in front of her eyes. He stood and watched her without saying a word. The silence lengthened.

'Have it your way, then,' he said quietly, and walked away.

* * *

All the pleasure of working in the studio seemed to have gone. For the rest of that week, whenever she spoke to Luke, her words sounded forced and unnatural, and Luke answered her politely, with none of the bantering and teasing of before.

After a day or two of this, Jeannie couldn't stand it any longer.

'What's the matter with you?' she asked Andrea. 'Have you and Luke had an argument? The atmosphere in here is like ice. I can't do any work!'

'I know,' Andrea muttered, 'the atmosphere's terrible. And yes, we had a bit of an argument. But it'll blow over.'

'Well, this is awful! I hate coming in and seeing the two of you scowling at each other. It spoils my whole day! Can't you make it up?'

'There's nothing to 'make up' really,' Andrea replied. 'Luke made some personal remarks about someone I like and I took exception to it, that's all.'

'You mean about Grant? What did he say?'

'That's none of your business — and since what he said was a lie in any case,

'I'm certainly not repeating it,' she said firmly.

'Was it anything to do with Grant being fired from Mattler Horne?' asked the younger girl hesitantly.

Andrea went cold. Did the whole world think he'd been fired except her?

'No,' she lied. 'Anyway, Grant was not fired. He resigned after a big fight with the management.'

'Is that what he told you?' Jeannie sounded doubtful. 'My friend Judy's a secretary there and she says he was fired for falsifying his expense account by hundreds of pounds! She said he's apparently been doing it for months.'

'That's just not true!' cried Andrea. 'Why is everyone saying such awful things about him? They're just jealous of his success. And I know you've never liked him so I suppose you just love spreading lies like that!'

'Oh, Andy, I'm not spreading lies, really I'm not.' Jeannie was distressed and embarrassed. 'It's just that every-one has been talking about it and I thought you knew.'

'It's a lie,' Andrea repeated stubbornly, her face burning.

'And anyway,' Jeannie continued quietly, 'you think I have no reason for disliking Grant. But I do. Just after you started seeing him, he came into the studio one day to wait for you and he started to . . . well, I mean, I had to push him away from me. It was awful. So now you know. I don't like him because he's a sleazy creep and I think you deserve someone a lot better, that's all.'

Andrea stared at her in horror, her mind racing. 'I don't believe you,' she whispered. 'Grant would never do something like that. He's too much of a gentleman.'

Jeannie turned away, tears in her eyes.

'Believe what you like,' she replied, 'I don't care. I wasn't going to tell you because I knew you wouldn't believe anything bad about your precious Grant. But it's true.'

Andrea stared at her computer screen and tried to focus on her work, but it was impossible. She decided she'd better tell Grant about the stories going around about his departure from Mattler Horne. That way he could confront the gossipers and put a stop to all the malicious rumours. If this went on, he wouldn't be able to find another job in advertising anywhere in Lymchester, where everyone seemed to know everything about everybody else.

But later that same afternoon, before she had the chance to speak to him, she had an unexpected phone call at the studio.

'Andrea? Lucy Carter here. How are you, my dear?'

'I — I'm fine, thank you,' she answered. What could Grant's mother possibly want to speak to her for?

She found out almost immediately. Mrs Carter was not one to beat about the bush.

'Andrea, dear, as I'm sure you know, Grant was practically forced to resign from that awful place he was working at — the people were dreadful, there was no way he could possibly stay there. Now, I know you're in the same sort of business, although not, of course, on quite the same, er, level as Grant, and I was wondering if there might be an opening for my son with your company?'

Andrea was dumbfounded. What on earth could she say? And how could this woman phone around trying to get a job for her son? Surely Grant would be furious if he knew what she was doing?

'Er, Mrs Carter, I don't think — that is, you know — we're a very small firm and the only two account executives we have are actually the owners of the business. I don't think they'd want to take on anyone new.'

'Well, you'll never know unless you ask, will you?' Mrs Carter went on silkily. 'Poor darling Grant is absolutely distraught about finding himself in this position. Of course, I know he could get a job just like that if he went up to London, but I've been trying to persuade him not to. I don't think London is the place for him at all.'

Well, at least we agree on one thing, thought Andrea.

'I don't know,' she told Mrs Carter, 'staff recruitment is really nothing to do with me, and Grant hasn't said he wants to work here anyway.'

'My dear, I know my son is very fond of you and I'm sure nothing would make him happier than to be working with you. Even though he would naturally be in a more senior position. But, of course, he is far too proud to ask you to put in a word on his behalf, which is why I am asking you myself.'

Andrea was startled. 'Does Grant know you're talking to me about this?'

'We-ell, he said he thought there might be a possible opening in your little agency, so I thought I'd just sound you out to get the — er — lay of the land. He wouldn't want to approach the powers that be completely cold, you know. An introduction from you might make all the difference.'

Andrea was silent for a moment.

'I'll see what I can do, Mrs Carter,' she said eventually. 'But I honestly don't think I can do much.'

'I know I can count on you to do your best for Grant, my dear.'

Andrea replaced the receiver, her thoughts whirling.

Grant working here at Market Media?

Her first, overpowering thought was — absolutely not.

She tried to imagine him working down the corridor from her and realised, with a sudden flash of clarity, that he just wouldn't fit in. She'd never seen Grant at work but she could picture him drifting through the day, issuing orders to his secretary in the most charming way, beguiling everyone around him to do his work for him, spending hours on business lunches with clients.

Exactly the sort of person Luke would make sarcastic comments about.

Market Media's new art director had

no time for the sort of people he called the Cocktail Charlies of the advertising world, men whose sole job seemed to be keeping clients well fed and entertained while the artists and copywriters did the hard work on the campaigns which brought results and kept the clients with the agency.

If Grant joined the firm, she knew it would be just a matter of time before Luke's bluntness would lead to all-out war between the two men.

The opinions he'd already expressed about Grant before he even knew him were bad enough.

She tried to picture Grant in Luke's office, probably sitting on the edge of the desk, chatting casually, making facetious remarks in his usual witty way, with Luke staring stonily at him and barking out replies which showed he thought Grant was a fool.

Oh no, she thought, I couldn't allow that to happen!

The atmosphere between her and Luke was not good, but with Grant in the same firm it would become impossible. There was no way she was ever going to ask the directors if they needed another account executive.

Abruptly she dialled Grant's number, to tell him about his mother's request.

But to her relief, Grant didn't answer. He's out, she thought, replacing the phone. I hope he's gone for an interview with someone who'll offer him a job. That would solve everything.

A New Campaign

For the next two days, there was no word from Grant. But when he finally phoned her at work one morning, he was exuberant, although he tried to pretend he was only mildly pleased.

'I've decided to accept an offer from Atherstone's,' he announced casually. 'They heard I was available and they seemed determined to have me. They wouldn't take no for an answer. So I've said I'll try it for a couple of months and see how it goes.'

'Atherstone's? That's wonderful! They do all the advertising for that enormous Freshfood chain, don't they?'

'That's just one of their larger accounts, but they do a lot of other things too. Wine, motor oil, a finance company, office equipment, all sorts. I'll be handling a couple of their smaller accounts at first but I expect I'll be offered something more juicy to get my teeth into once they've seen what I can do.'

'Oh, Grant, I'm so pleased for you. I was so worried.'

'Little silly, you should have known something would turn up.'

Andrea decided not to mention his mother's phone call after all.

'Have you told your mother about your new job?' she asked cautiously.

'Yes, I phoned her at once. Funnily enough, it turns out that she knows old man Atherstone — they belonged to the same tennis club about a hundred years ago. Small world, isn't it?'

Another of his mother's phone calls, bearing fruit this time, Andrea thought, and was immediately angry with herself for the disloyal thought.

Of course Grant had got this job on the strength of his own experience and obvious ability.

'Mind you, it always helps having some kind of connection with the top brass,' he continued cheerfully. 'Now, am I going to see you this evening?'

'I promised Barbara I'd look in — I haven't seen her for ages. I can't disappoint her.'

'Ah, Barbara — now there's a really nice girl. Tell you what, I'll pick you up from her place at about nine o'clock. That should give you girls time for a good gossip, and then you and I can go out for a bite to eat.'

'Lovely.' She smiled, happy that he was happy. 'See you tonight.'

'Can I have a word with you, Andrea?'

Luke stood in the doorway to his office. He motioned her to follow him in, waited until she had sat down and then closed the door, something he almost never did.

'What's the matter?' she asked flatly, facing him across his desk which was strewn with layouts. Things had improved somewhat, but there was still a chilly gulf between them.

'It looks as though there might be another big job coming up,' he said. 'Remember Mike Cooper?'

'At that party? The American? Yes, of course.'

'Well, apart from being full of charm, he also owns a small computer company called Compuvision. Now he's gone into partnership with a much bigger firm with connections in England and Japan, and they're wanting to launch a big advertising campaign. Mike is bringing two of his associates around for a meeting this afternoon and I'd like you to sit in on it.'

'Must I?' she asked faintly. 'I don't know what to say to those executive types.'

'That's OK. I just want you there to sit in the corner looking pretty and keeping quiet.'

'If you think — ' she burst out and then caught his eye. He was grinning at her with his old mischievous twinkle.

'Well, anyway, I can't see what use I'll be,' she went on. 'I don't know much about computers and technology.'

'We're not going to talk about computers as such. We're going to be bouncing around a few ideas to spark off a good advertising campaign. And as I have great respect for your ideas, I'd appreciate your input.'

Andrea's heart lifted and suddenly all the coldness between them fell away.

'OK,' she said, 'I'll be there.'

'With a small smile on your face?'

'I suppose so.'

She couldn't help a big grin breaking out as she left his office, and went back to her desk humming. I'll probably sit at the table with nothing to say anyhow, she thought ruefully. I always think of smart answers long after they're needed.

But she attacked a layout for health food with renewed enthusiasm.

★ ★ ★

The meeting wasn't at all as she'd imagined it would be. Mike's casual introduction of his partners and his instant recognition of her dispelled all her anxieties about being there.

'Aha, the awesome Andrea, ace

assistant!' he said warmly as he took both her hands in his. 'Glad to see you again. These are Graham and Mark, from our marketing division. Boys, this is Andrea Ross, and watch out, she's a sharp cookie.'

Luke interrupted in a businesslike voice. 'OK, Mike, tell us what this is all about.'

They sat around the polished teak boardroom table and sheets of figures were passed around. At first, the talk was all about unit numbers and delivery dates and Andrea found herself drifting off as she stared at the oil paintings on the wall. One was of a mountain peak and she suddenly thought back to that Saturday on Mount Ayliff when Luke had come so close to taking her in an embrace. She flushed as she remembered the longing for him that had swept over her.

'Andrea? What do you think?'

Mike's voice brought her back sharply to the present. 'I'm sorry?'

'The launch date. Does five weeks

from now suit you? Can you folks get a press and TV campaign together in that time?'

'If Luke thinks we can,' she replied, glancing at Luke who was doodling on a pad in front of him.

'That would depend on how soon we can agree on the theme of the campaign,' he interjected. 'If we come up with something and you like it, Mike, then fine. But if there's a lot of sending stuff back for changes, then that can hold up the whole works.'

'Luke, as far as we're concerned, you'll have a free hand. You've produced nothing but good work and I have complete faith that this campaign will be another award winner! There's just one thing.'

'Yes?'

'We need to be sure that nothing leaks out about the campaign until it actually appears in the press and on TV. How is your security here at Market Media?'

'We're aware of the need for secrecy,' said Luke. 'Nobody comes into the studio, not even the other staff. You needn't worry about anything getting out. Now then, what has the main thrust of your marketing been up until now?'

'Our selling point has always been that we manufacture a very economic computer, good value for money, that sort of thing,' said Mike. 'We still want to be seen as good value, of course, but we've come up with a totally new design, very rounded, very different from anything presently available. We're also going to be making some of the fastest computers on the market. Plus — and this is where we're going to knock socks off our competitors — we're bringing them out in ten different colours. Different shades of red, blue, green. Even gold and silver.'

'That sounds great!' Andrea was suddenly excited by a vision of a futuristic office with matching office furniture, perhaps blue computer, blue desk, blue chairs. 'You won't want to keep the same name then, will you?'

'No, definitely not. New product, new name. We're hoping you can help us there too. We need something snappy, something people will remember.'

'What was the focus of your previous advertising campaign?' Luke was making notes as they spoke.

'We featured a secretary dressed in a kilt with a Scots accent. You know, canny Scot, knows a good thing when she sees it, that sort of thing.'

Luke pulled a face. 'I think we can do a bit better than that.'

'The viewers loved it,' said Mike huffily. 'Mind you, she had stunning legs and a very short kilt — that helped! Well, I'm sure you two will come up with something a bit different. I look forward to seeing your suggestions, and remember, you can be as original as you like. I'd like to see something completely mind-boggling. I propose that we meet again three days from now and have a look at what you've thought up?'

Three days, thought Andrea. Mike really means business. She walked back to the studio, wondering how to come up with a mind-boggling, completely different, award-winning idea to sell computers by then.

$\star$ $\star$ $\star$

Back at her desk she put paper into her printer and then settled down to work at some ideas for the new campaign.

As usual, her mind went completely blank. Her second cup of coffee at her elbow, her sketch pad in front of her, and she could think of absolutely nothing appropriate.

'We need a name,' she muttered. 'Once we've got a name for this new company then the rest will follow.'

Jeannie looked across at her sympathetically. 'Leave it for a bit,' she suggested. 'Go for a walk or something.'

'I can't spare the time,' Andrea said with a sigh. 'We've only got three days to come up with some decent preliminary sketches.' She walked through to Luke's office. 'Any bright ideas coming through?' she queried. 'I can't think of a thing.'

His desk was littered with pieces of paper covered with scribbles, all with black lines drawn through them.

'I've had lots of ideas,' he answered, 'but most of them are useless. I think we'll have to do this systematically. Sit down and think of a name first. Write down absolutely anything that comes into your head and remember that these new computers are brightly coloured instead of boring old grey. That's quite a point to remember. And a whole new shape. And then remember that the new company is a tie-up of Japanese and American technology. Maybe the name should reflect that. Maybe not. I don't know.'

They sat in silence for a while, with one or other of them scribbling something every now and then.

Luke ran his hand through his hair in exasperation and sighed.

'Printmaster, Compu-print, Digiview, Computa-king. No good. What have you got?'

'Mine are just as bad. Dojo-print — '

225

'Dojo-print? What's that supposed to mean?'

'Dojo. Isn't that something to do with karate or judo? I thought it sounded vaguely Japanese.'

They both started laughing.

'And how do you operate these Dojo-prints? Slice them with the side of your hand or kick them with your foot?'

'Maybe you have to shout 'Hai-ah' every time you start them up!' She giggled.

Luke stood up. 'OK, that's enough for now. Let's go home and start again tomorrow. Something is bound to occur to one of us overnight.'

With a start, Andrea realised that it was after eight o'clock.

Everyone else had long since left for the day and the office was dark and deserted. Grant would be expecting to pick her up at Barbara's soon.

'Join me for steak and chips?' Luke asked casually as they went down in the lift.

'I'd love to, but I can't. I've promised

to visit a girlfriend and I'm late already,' she answered regretfully.

'Let me run you to wherever you're going then,' he offered. 'It's the least I can do at this time of night.'

She gave him directions to Barbara's flat and waited while he scooped a pile of books and papers off the passenger seat to make room for her. The van felt warm and familiar. As Andrea sat down, her feet tangled with something lying on the floor.

'Sorry, let me get this out of the way too,' he said, tossing an old rucksack into the back of the van. 'I was walking last weekend and haven't got round to putting this back where it belongs.'

His arm brushed her leg and instantly she felt as though her whole body were on fire. What is it with this man, she thought.

'Where did you go?' she asked, her voice shaking slightly. She averted her face, thankful that it was dark in the van.

'Forris Crag. It's just a strenuous walk, not a climb. But it has some wonderful views from the top. Pity you weren't up there with me,' he said quietly. 'You'd have loved it.'

She could tell that he was gazing at her intently but she bit her lip and said nothing.

'If I absolutely promise not to mention Grant Carter's name, would you come out walking with me again one day?'

She was surprised to hear herself say, 'Yes, I'd love to.'

'Good, let's make it this Saturday then,' he said before she could change her mind.

What on earth have I agreed to, she thought wildly, but she suddenly realised that there was nothing she wanted more than to spend the day with Luke up in the mountains, far away from everything else in the world.

Her emotions in turmoil, she muttered good night and fled up the steps to Barbara's flat.

★ ★ ★

'What kept you so long?' asked Barbara, pouring coffee for them both. 'Is that monster overworking you again?'

'Well, I'm certainly working hard, but it's no hardship. I enjoy it.'

She described her day to Barbara who, as usual, wanted to hear all thedetails.

She wasn't sure why, but for some reason she'd not told Barbara about her climb with Luke on Mount Ayliff and decided not to mention his latest invitation either. Explaining her feelings for Luke would just be too complicated. If I could only explain them to myself in the first place, she thought ruefully.

'Grant's picking me up here at nine o'clock,' she said. 'Thank goodness he's found another job. Did I mention it?'

'No, but he did!' Barbara smiled. 'He popped in yesterday to tell me.'

'Did he?'

Andrea was momentarily puzzled and a bit hurt. Fancy Grant telling Barbara before he told her, when he knew how worried she'd been.

'Grant's been so kind. He often comes in just to keep me company for half an hour or so. Especially since he's been out of work. You don't mind, do you?'

'Of course not,' Andrea said quickly. 'I'm just glad the two of you have hit it off so well.'

'You're always the main topic of conversation anyway,' said Barbara cheerfully. 'He never stops talking about you and how talented you are. I'm sure your ears must burn sometimes.'

Just then the buzzer sounded and Grant was standing on the doorstep, a bottle of champagne in his hand.

'Greetings, ladies,' he announced. 'Andy — glasses, please. We three will celebrate my new appointment in a style befitting a future director of Atherstone's.'

Andrea couldn't help a wry smile. Already he was imagining himself sitting in the biggest office, surrounded by underlings who jumped to his every command. Never mind that he hadn't even started work there yet.

They finished the champagne with the two girls cheerfully proposing toasts to Grant's new job and his future success.

Looking at his lean body draped carelessly over the sofa, his easy smile flashing with confidence, Andrea hoped this would be a new beginning for him. I won't say anything about all that gossip, it will only hurt him, she thought.

Grant raised his glass and toasted them both.

'Here's to the beauty I see before me, which brightens my life. Long may you continue to do so!'

He winked at Andrea but leaned over to ruffle Barbara's hair in what could almost have been an intimate caress. The blind girl flushed with pleasure.

'Isn't he awful, Andrea?' she said, clutching at Grant's hand and smacking it lightly. 'Pay no attention to him.'

What is he playing at, wondered Andrea. Is he doing that so Barbara doesn't feel left out? Is he trying to make me jealous? She stared across at the two of them, wondering why she wasn't more upset. She decided that it was because she was mature enough to see Grant's casual caress as nothing other than a friendly gesture to Barbara who was, after all, her best friend.

She jumped up from her chair.

'I'm starving,' she announced. 'Are we going to take Barbara out for a meal with us, Grant?'

'No, I'm much too comfortable. Why don't you two women find something for us to eat right here? I'm sure Barbara won't mind,' he answered lazily.

'Of course not.' Barbara led the way into her tiny kitchen with Andrea following. 'I've nothing much to eat,' she apologised, feeling around in the refrigerator. 'If I'd known you'd stay I would have done some shopping. I was just going to make myself a sandwich for my supper.'

'Just as well we've stayed then,' said

Andrea, beating eggs to scramble them and cutting bread for toast. 'You've got to eat properly, Barbs, or you'll fade away.'

'I should definitely come for supper more often, in that case,' said Grant casually. He was lounging against the door frame as he watched their activities. 'This girl is a great cook, Andy. You should taste her fried chicken.'

'Er . . . yes, I know she's a good cook,' said Andrea, her voice betraying her confusion.

'Grant was kind enough to stay for supper last week and help me finish some leftovers,' Barbara explained.

'And your chocolate cream pud! That was terrific. You should give Andy the recipe. Maybe it will inspire her to use her kitchen for something besides boiling water.'

As they ate, Andrea was silent. She knew she should have been pleased to hear that Grant and Barbara were becoming such good friends, but why hadn't Grant said anything about them having a meal together? Did he think Andrea would be angry?

And Barbara was usually so open, so why hadn't she mentioned inviting Grant to stay for something to eat? Had she not been as honest with Andrea as she'd thought?

She looked at Barbara's glowing face, turned towards Grant as she listened to him joking with her. She's really beautiful tonight, Andrea thought, and with a sudden shock she knew why.

Barbara was in love with Grant. And Grant seemed to be encouraging her to fall for him . . .

Andrea studied Grant's mobile, smiling face, and listened to his mellifluous voice teasing her friend. Any girl would fall for him, she thought, just as I did. He's just so darned charming, he can't help attracting just about every woman he meets, even Barbara.

For the first time, the thought struck her that Grant was just a bit too handsome and well-dressed for her taste. His mouth was too quick to smile in that crooked, little-boy way. And she was suddenly irritated by the fact that his hair was so well-cut and styled, his clothes always so immaculate. Why can't he be rougher, a bit less polished? Why can't he be more like a real man?

Andrea tried to stifle a picture of Luke on the mountain, his hair blowing in the wind and his faded blue jeans stuffed into his climbing boots.

'Like what you see?' Grant felt her critical gaze and turned to her with a disarming wink.

'Oh — er, of course.' She got up and cleared the plates before Barbara could move. 'You two stay there, I'll wash up.'

Andrea heard them chatting and laughing while she was in the kitchen and when she went back they were sitting close together on the sofa.

She suggested a game of Trivial Pursuit and the next hour passed amidst a lot of laughter and banter between Grant and Barbara. More and more, as the evening progressed,

Andrea felt completely detached, as though she were a stranger watching the scene from far away. She tried to analyse what she felt and the slow realisation dawned on her that she felt nothing.

I don't care if he flirts with everyone he meets, I just don't care.

I don't love Grant and I don't think I ever have.

As soon as she'd framed the words in her mind, she was flooded with a heady sense of relief. No more waiting hopefully for the phone to ring. No more dressing up to please him and going to smart, expensive restaurants. No more trying to impress his mother. She'd be free to go running, climbing, join a gym, anything she felt like, without having to consider Grant's preferences.

How could I have thought he was the right man for me, she wondered.

This thought flooded her with such elation and happiness that she felt like smiling kindly at Grant and giving him her blessing, but she sipped her coffee and considered the two people sitting opposite her.

I wonder if he feels anything for Barbara, she thought. Her blindness doesn't seem to worry him at all and she's so lovely, any man would be lucky to have her for a wife. And she's so calm and sweet-natured, Grant's mother would love her. If the two of them could get together, things would be perfect. But he's probably just flirting, as usual.

*　*　*

That evening, Andrea and Grant left Barbara's together and Grant ran Andrea home. As his car drew up outside her flat and he started to open his own door, she said quickly, 'I'm not going to offer you coffee, Grant, I've got to be up at the crack of dawn to get to work tomorrow.'

'Oh! Are you working on something new?'

Remembering Luke's obsession with

secrecy, she said, 'No, I just have a job that I need to finish in a hurry.'

'So why the rush?' he asked, his finger tracing a line up the inside of her bare arm. He raised her hand and planted little kisses on the tips of her fingers, gazing into her eyes.

Any other evening, this would have melted Andrea's resolve, but tonight she felt completely detached and unable to respond.

So this is what it's like to fall out of love, she thought, picking up her bag and getting out of the car.

'Good night, Grant, I'll phone you,' she said, and walked up her path. She felt almost guilty that she'd said nothing to him about her change of feelings. I'll speak to him over the weekend when there's more time, she decided. She hadn't the energy for a big scene that night.

She hadn't given computers a thought all evening, but as she made ready for bed, she started to go over possible names in her mind and found she couldn't switch off.

A Lucky Escape for Andrea

Sitting on the top of the bus going to work the following day, Andrea glanced idly at a billboard advertising washing powder.

'*Put the colour back in your washing!*' it declared. And all at once an idea for a television campaign started to form in her mind.

What if they filmed everything in black and white to start with — an office scene — and slowly a blue light floats in through the door and settles on an empty desk? The office staff stand around watching in amazement as the blue light turns into a beautiful blue computer. And then suddenly the whole scene switches to bright colour.

It could be so effective and it would really bring home the idea of coloured office equipment.

Her thoughts raced on and by the

time she got to the studio she knew exactly how her idea would work and couldn't wait to tell Luke.

He was already at his desk, and grinned triumphantly when he saw her.

'Spectrum!' he announced. 'How's that for a name?'

'That's perfect! It means the whole range . . . '

'The whole range of everything. So it's the whole spectrum of colours, and could also mean it can do the whole spectrum of programmes or whatever.'

'It's great. And listen, I have an idea for the campaign that would really fit in with that.'

She explained her idea, the words tumbling out in her excitement.

Luke quickly caught on and started adding his own ideas.

'A whole series of TV advertisements, featuring a different coloured computer each time, each with a different office setting. And the print adverts for newspapers, we could do those all in black and white, too, with the computer making just one bright splash of colour. I think we've got it. Good girl!'

He started to give her a quick hug of appreciation, but somehow his arm stayed where it was and he tightened his grip. This feels so right, she thought, and had to resist an overwhelming impulse to nestle against his hard male chest and stay in the circle of his embrace for the rest of the morning.

She slipped out from under his arm and said shakily, 'We have a lot of work to do.'

'Andy,' his voice was unsteady, 'I think you and I have to talk.'

The naked emotion on his face told her just what it was that he wanted to talk about!

He feels the same as I do! But I'm not ready for this, she thought. I haven't broken things off with Grant yet. I need time.

She turned to Luke and said brightly, 'Right. You prepare a few print media roughs for Mike and I'll get busy with a story-board for the TV adverts. Then perhaps we can compare notes at lunch-time.'

She could feel his eyes boring a hole in her back as she left the room.

But as she sat down at her desk and set to work, she was smiling to herself. Somehow everything was going to work out and Luke was going to be there for her when she'd sorted things out with Grant.

★   ★   ★

Jeannie was out of the studio on an errand, and Andrea was down on her hands and knees, searching for some new printer paper at the bottom of the cupboard, when a cool clear voice above her head asked, 'Is Luke Sullivan anywhere around?'

She looked up to see a tall, elegant woman leaning back against her desk, studying her with amusement. Diamonds sparkled at the woman's ears and she seemed to be dressed entirely in fur — fur coat, fur-topped boots and a Russian-style fur hat nestled above a smooth dark bob.

Andrea sprang to her feet in dismay, dusting her knees.

'You must be Andrea,' said the woman. 'My name's Rosalind Kent. Luke's mentioned you. You're his little graphic artist, aren't you?'

'Little graphic artist' indeed! 'Yes,' she said stiffly, hating Rosalind Kent on sight. 'Luke's in his office, over there.'

'I'll just surprise him then,' said Rosalind. 'Tempt him out for some lunch. You know what he's like, such a workaholic. But I'll make him an offer he simply cannot refuse.'

She drifted over to Luke's office and opened the door, gurgling with laughter as she did so. Andrea couldn't hear the rest of the conversation but five minutes later Luke followed her out, smiling and shrugging into his jacket.

'I've got to go out for a while, Andy,' he said, taking Rosalind Kent's arm and guiding her out between the studio tables. 'If I'm not back by the time you

243

leave, lock up for me, will you?'

So that was Rosalind, the lady of the flowers and the theatre tickets. She was beautiful and chic and she looked as though she belonged on Luke's arm.

He must like older women, Andrea thought dully, and was shocked at the intense jealousy she felt as she watched them leave.

She stuck out her tongue at their retreating backs and felt childishly relieved. Idiot, she thought.

★　★　★

Over the next three days the studio was a whirl of activity. Joe and Martin were called in to discuss the project, with Andrea sitting in on all the meetings. These took up more time than she expected and she was busy until late every evening, never getting home before midnight.

She drafted and re-drafted layouts, with Luke suggesting changes and demanding additions: make the computer bigger, change the angle of the desks, put more people in the picture.

'Gosh, he's never satisfied, is he?' said Jeannie sympathetically. 'Maybe you should remind him that this campaign was your idea, not his.'

'No, he's right as usual,' muttered Andrea. 'It looks better his way.'

Finally, an hour before the Friday meeting scheduled with Mike and his associates, everything was ready, with the series of layouts and story-boards mounted on black card and covered in plastic.

'OK. Jeannie, mind the fort. Andy and I will only be a couple of hours.'

Andrea followed him out of the studio, their pile of layouts in a big folder. Tweedledum met them in the passage outside the lift.

'Ah, Mr Sullivan and Miss Ross.' He beamed at them. 'Off to see our new clients, are you? Is that the art work?'

'Not the finished stuff, just the roughs,' answered Luke. 'Andrea's worked out some pretty impressive ideas for them.'

Andrea's cheeks burned at his words

and a glow of pure happiness pulsed through her body. Praise from Luke was praise indeed.

'That was generous of you,' she blurted out as they descended in the lift.

'Not at all. Most of the ideas were yours. I just smoothed a few of the rough edges,' he said. 'Don't sell yourself short, Andy — you know you're good. Although, of course,' he added mischievously, 'you've improved no end under my guidance.'

'Oh — you!' She grinned at him. It was true, her work had improved enormously and it was all down to him.

This time the meeting was in Mike's office across town.

'I think we should splash out on a taxi, don't you?' suggested Luke. He was in excellent spirits. 'Mike's going to go for this campaign in a big way. It's a winner.'

★ ★ ★

It was. Mike and his colleagues were delighted with the whole concept and

246

Andrea and Luke were given the go-ahead to set up the TV filming and to finish the work for the media.

'You thought we were busy this past week? Just wait until Monday,' said Luke as they returned to the studio. 'We've been given a really punishing schedule. Mike's talking of the campaign starting three weeks from now, nationwide.'

'We can't possibly manage that!' Andrea exclaimed. 'He's crazy!'

'We can and he is,' said Luke equably. 'But we'll manage. We'll just have to persuade Martin and Joe to drop everything else and concentrate on us. In the meantime, we'll forget all about it until Monday. Are you ready for Forris Crag tomorrow?'

'Oh yes,' she replied. A good, windy day on the mountains was just what she needed. Whether she could withstand a day alone with Luke without her defences crumbling was another matter.

'I'll call for you at about eight in the morning, all right? And don't worry about bringing anything to eat. I'll see to everything. Just make sure you're wearing . . . '

'Sensible walking shoes and a warm sweater! Right.'

'You're learning.'

She hadn't thought of Grant since the last time she'd seen him and she suddenly realised that he'd more than likely phone her that evening. He hated to stay in on a Friday and would be expecting her to be ready to go with him to wherever he decided.

I've got to tell him how I feel and I know I'm just putting off the moment when I break with him, she thought guiltily. But I can't face a heavy emotional scene. Not tonight.

She went home, took the receiver off the hook, and fell into an exhausted, dreamless sleep.

★   ★   ★

Jessie bounded ahead, leaping from boulder to boulder, and kept looking back over her shoulder as if to say, 'Come on, you two, can't you keep up?'

'That dog thinks she's a mountain goat,' grumbled Andrea, who was beginning to feel the ache in her legs. 'Isn't it time for a rest? We should take a break and admire the view!'

'At the top. We're almost there, just another ten minutes.'

Luke strode on without stopping, his long muscular legs making short work of the steep path that led to the top of Forris Crag. His hair was a tangled mane blowing about his tanned face, and his expression held something almost harsh and elemental that Andrea had never seen before.

He could be more considerate, she thought crossly, he knows I'm not a hot-shot climber like he is. It's almost as though he's forgotten I'm here. He shouldn't expect me to keep up the pace he does. It would serve him right if I fell and broke my leg, then he'd *have* to wait.

These and other thoughts swirled

resentfully through her mind as she struggled on. It was four hours since they'd left the camper van in the valley far below, and they'd stopped for only one short rest, sharing a cup of hot sweet tea from his flask. Her cheeks flushed and glowing, she forced her legs to continue and reached the summit only a few minutes after Luke.

He straddled a rock, gazing out across the scene below and turned to her with a triumphant grin.

'Worth it?' he asked happily.

'Yes,' she panted, her hands on her knees. 'Definitely!'

He laughed exultantly. 'I knew you'd love it.'

His hand rested on Jessie's head and the magnificent dog turned her golden eyes on him in appreciation.

'Jessie's a great climber, aren't you, old girl?'

'She's got four legs, she should be,' said Andrea. 'I'd do better with a couple more myself! What have you got in that pack of yours? Anything to eat?'

'Let's find a spot out of the wind for lunch.'

They settled down on a soft, grassy patch behind a wall of brown granite.

Andrea leaned against a rock and stretched, luxuriating in the peace and silence. Nothing but the sigh of the wind and the call of birds somewhere in the distance, and the sound of Luke unpacking his old canvas rucksack.

She sat up guiltily.

'Can I help you to do anything?'

'Just relax — everything's ready. Madam may now take a little lunch.'

On the rock in front of them he had spread out a veritable feast consisting of crisp rolls, sliced ham, cheeses and salads.

Her eyes widened. 'Great! You believe in doing things properly, don't you?'

'Oh, I sometimes have quite good ideas. Cheers!'

Everything seemed to taste better than any food she'd eaten for a long time, and as they ate and drank in companionable silence, Andrea idly watched bees hovering busily above the heather and marvelled at the country spread out beneath them.

They were so high that she could see three different villages far away in the distance, and the hills at the foot of the mountain looked like molehills below them. Pretty little white clouds scudded across the arc of azure-blue sky above.

Slowly, the warmth of their sheltered spot seeped into her body and she lay back, totally at peace with the world.

'Luke,' she murmured sleepily, 'we don't have to rush to go back, do we? There's plenty of time to get down from the mountain before dark.'

When he didn't reply she glanced across at him. His eyes had closed and he was asleep, his features completely relaxed.

She studied his face objectively. His thick eyebrows sometimes gave him a forbidding look, but there were smile lines that she'd never noticed before around his eyes and mouth and a humorous twist to his lips.

She wasn't sure whether to be annoyed that he'd fallen asleep, or to be flattered that he could relax so completely in her company.

Before she could decide which, the scent of the warm heather and the humming of the bees overcame her senses and she drifted off herself.

When she awoke, it was to find Jessie's hairy face close to her own, her tail thumping out a message that she was tired of lying around waiting for something to happen.

'OK, OK,' she grumbled, 'I hear you. Now tell your master.'

Luke's eyes were open and he was looking across at her sleepily.

'Don't worry, I don't blame you for having forty winks,' he said. 'Fresh air does terrible things to a girl who's not used to it.'

'That's rich, coming from someone who was practically snoring the minute he finished lunch!' she joked. 'Isn't it time we were going?'

Luke glanced up at the sky and

immediately jerked to his feet.

'You're right! Look at the weather.'

While they'd slept, the sun and the warmth had disappeared and the pretty white clouds had closed ranks and become a low mass, grey and threatening.

Andrea dug into her pack for her parka, slipping it on hastily.

'This is just what we didn't need — bad weather,' muttered Luke, cramming the remains of their lunch into his rucksack. 'Sorry, Andy, it looks as though we'll have to get down as fast as we can.'

She shrugged on her own rucksack and meekly followed him back along the path they'd come up by.

'I was intending to take the other route down, to show you the view from the other side,' he said over his shoulder. 'But I'm not taking any chances with conditions like these.'

Privately Andrea didn't think the clouds looked too bad. What's a bit of rain, she thought; it's not as though I've never got wet while walking before. And there's a perfectly good path. But she caught the sense of urgency in Luke's pace and did her best to keep up with him.

A light rain began to fall and she shivered in spite of her waterproof jacket. Who would have thought the weather could change so quickly?

Soon a thick wet mist was swirling around them, cutting the visibility to only a few feet. With the bright red of Luke's cagoule like a beacon in front her, she slipped and slid down the path as she followed him, wiping the rain from her eyes as she went.

Once, she stumbled and would have fallen if he hadn't swung round and caught her arm.

She smiled at him gratefully. 'Sorry,' she panted, 'I lost my footing. I'm just not used to running down mountains like this!'

'Take my hand,' said Luke abruptly. 'Don't let go.'

He gripped her icy hand in his and

slowed his steps to match her own, patiently helping her over the fast-running streams that had appeared from nowhere once the rain started.

Her socks inside her walking shoes were soon squelching uncomfortably and her sopping jeans flapped around her ankles and clung to her frozen legs. The path down seemed endless. Even Jessie lost her enthusiasm and plodded ahead of them both, her coat matted and muddy.

After what seemed like hours, Luke came to an abrupt halt and peered ahead into the wall of mist, listening.

'What is it?' queried Andrea, her teeth chattering.

'I just want to check that we're still on the right path,' he said. 'This last couple of hundred metres hasn't looked familiar but the mist sometimes does strange things.' He turned to her. 'How are you doing?'

'I'm fine,' she assured him. 'Best Saturday I've had in ages. Beats watching the laundry go round and round!'

'That's my girl.' He squeezed her hand. 'Stay here for one moment; I'm going to take a look down to the left. If we are where I think we are, we're only about twenty minutes from the van. Don't move from the path.'

'I won't.'

She stayed perfectly still, watching his reassuringly large form disappear into the mist.

After a few minutes, she realised how weary she was and how stiff her legs felt. She looked around for somewhere to rest, not too far from the path so she would spot Luke when he returned. Through the mist, she saw a large rock and walked over to it, slinging her pack off her back and sitting down thankfully.

What happened next was a terrifying blur of noise and sensations.

Suddenly there was a rumbling sound which seemed to come from all around her, and all at once the world turned upside down. It was as if a giant hand had picked her up and tossed her roughly down the mountain. She was conscious of her body falling, banging against rocks and slipping down over mud while her nerveless fingers tried hopelessly to grasp anything in her path to stop her from sliding down the hill. All around her boomed a monstrous noise of tumbling rocks and stones.

After long minutes she came to a bruising and abrupt halt against an outcrop of rocks and lay motionless. The mountain was eerily still, the only sound that of the steadily falling rain.

Her first thought was one of relief that she was alive. Feeling curiously numb, she slowly moved her fingers and drew up her legs. Nothing seemed to be broken, so she tried to raise herself on to her elbow, but the world swam giddily before her eyes and she sank back against the rock, gasping.

She didn't know how long she'd been lying there before she heard Luke shouting her name through the mist and heard the crunching of his boots as he came half leaping, half running down the slope towards her.

'I'm over here!' She tried to shout but her voice came out as a croak.

Then she felt herself being lifted up in Luke's arms and clutched against his chest in a vice-like embrace.

Everything will be all right now, she thought dreamily.

'You're alive, you're alive,' he muttered, burying his face in her neck. 'Thank goodness. You're alive.'

He pulled her into an upright position.

'Are you all right?' Desperately his eyes searched her face.

'I think so,' she said shakily. 'I just feel dizzy. My leg hurts.'

'You fool, I told you to stay on the path.' His voice shook, whether from anger or some other emotion she couldn't tell. 'The whole side of the mountain went down in a massive rockfall — and took you with it. I thought I'd lost you for ever.'

'I knew you'd find me,' she said with a small smile. She wanted to say a lot more, but it was all too much of an effort.

She felt herself being gathered in his arms and nestled her head thankfully against the warm security of his chest. The last thing she was aware of was the rhythmic thud of his steps as he carried her down the mountain.

Betrayal!

Andrea woke to find herself in a strange bed, with someone she vaguely recognised bending over her.

'It's Dr Anderson, my dear.'

'What are you doing here?' Her mouth felt as though it was full of cotton wool.

'You had a nasty fall on the mountain this afternoon. Your young man was so worried about you he practically hijacked me to get me here, but I don't think you've any bones broken, nor concussion.'

The elderly doctor straightened up and turned to Luke who, she now noticed, was standing behind him.

'I'd say she's been a lucky young woman,' the doctor said, closing his bag. 'She'll have some painful bruises for a couple of days but apart from that, there's nothing wrong with her that a good night's sleep won't cure.'

He let himself out and the door clicked shut behind him.

Andrea gazed up at Luke, trying to remember what had happened.

'Where am I?'

'At my house. In my spare bedroom.'

'How did I get here? Oh!' She flushed hotly as she realised that someone had removed her wet clothes. Someone had dressed her in this garment she was now wearing. Raising her arm slightly, she saw she was clad in one of Luke's flannel shirts.

'Was this — I mean — did you?' She gave him a look of such dismay that he burst out laughing and sat down on her bed.

'That shirt looks very good on you,' he said lightly. 'It was no trouble. You can thank me later.'

She gazed at him speechlessly, waves of embarrassment washing over her.

'Don't worry. I asked Mrs Jones, my next-door neighbour, to come in and get you ready for bed. And I'm sure you would have been wearing clean underwear in case of an accident, so I don't think you need to be ashamed of anything.'

Despite herself, she giggled weakly.

Luke leaned over her and cupped her face in his hands.

How odd, his hands are always warm, she thought.

'You gave me a terrible fright,' he said roughly. 'I still can't believe you're all in one piece.'

'Oh, I'm tougher than I look,' she said, basking in the warmth of his concern.

His hand strayed to her forehead and brushed back her hair, gently twisting a stray strand around his finger. His eyes never left hers. Andrea lay totally still, transfixed by the feeling that he was looking into her very soul.

'Yeah, a real tough cookie.' He broke the mood abruptly and sat up. 'Are you ready for something to eat? And after that it will be time to sleep for you, Miss Ross.'

Alone in his spare room, Andrea looked around her curiously. The furniture was solid and functional, the walls bare of ornaments or pictures. A guitar leaned against one wall and what looked like a tent was rolled up in a corner. Her eye fell on a small silver-framed photograph on the bed-side table, and she turned it towards her.

Luke laughed at her from out of the picture, his arm around a tall, smiling woman with smooth, dark hair. It was Rosalind Kent. Andrea felt a sharp stab of disappointment. Don't be silly, she told herself, you knew about Rosalind and Luke, you knew he didn't come home to sit alone with Jessie every evening.

When Luke came back into the room he was carrying a tray that had on it a steaming bowl of hot soup.

'Sit up,' he said and plumped the pillows behind her. 'Get some of this inside you and you'll feel much better.'

The soup smelled delicious but

Andrea found that lifting the spoon to her mouth was an exhausting business. She collapsed back against the pillows and shook her head weakly.

'Thanks, but I don't feel like anything to eat.'

'Nonsense. I'll help you. You must have something.'

He lifted the spoon and fed her as tenderly as a baby, even wiping her chin when she spilled a drop. She was hazily content to let him do this, watching his face as he concentrated on the job of feeding her.

Is this really happening, she thought in wonder, obediently swallowing the soup as he raised it to her mouth. Lying in this bed felt like a warm delicious dream from which she did not want to awaken.

'All done.' He removed the bowl of soup but stayed where he was, sitting on the bed. Then his face clouded into brooding lines and he grasped her hand tightly in his.

'Andy, what happened today was my

fault. I can't forgive myself for getting you into such a dangerous situation. I keep imagining finding you lying dead at the bottom of the mountain . . . ' His voice trailed off and he covered his face with his hands.

'But it wasn't your fault that the weather changed,' she protested. 'The whole thing was a freak accident. If anyone's to blame, I am. I shouldn't have left the path. I didn't realise that the rock was so close to the edge of the slope.'

'I think I must be cursed.' His voice was muffled. 'I kept thinking, first Hailey and now you. I don't think I could bear it if anything happened to you.'

'What happened to Hailey?' she asked quietly.

She'd realised that Luke must have somehow been involved in her death, ever since Mike had spoken about her at the cocktail party.

'Did she have a fall while she was up in the mountains climbing with you?'

'How do you know about Hailey?' he asked her bleakly. 'Did Mike tell you?'

266

'Not really. He mentioned that she had an accident — I just guessed she was with you.'

There was a long silence.

'That was the problem. She wasn't with me,' he said slowly. 'At one time, Hailey and I used to leave New York and get away to climb together almost every weekend. She was good, but she was never good enough to tackle the north face of Eagles Nest. That weekend of the blizzard, she wanted to join me when I went climbing and I refused to take her. I told her she'd never manage the route I was planning to do and with the weather not looking so good, I wasn't going to take any chances. We ended up having a huge fight and I walked out.'

'So, how did she get there, then? Did you change your mind?'

'Not at all. The silly woman followed me on her own.'

'Didn't you know she was on the mountain?'

'Not until the weather started closing

in and I turned back. Then I spotted her going up a crevasse next to a sheer rock face some distance from where I was. I saw this little figure, dressed in yellow, climbing slowly upwards. Hailey always wore bright yellow climbing gear; you could recognise her a mile away.'

He stopped talking, and Andrea wondered if he'd thought better of telling her the story, but after a minute he continued.

'I couldn't believe my eyes, and when I shouted to her I could hear her laughing at me from across the gorge. I remember the sound travelled so well. I could hardly see her face but I could hear her laugh.'

He paused.

'Anyway, I waved to her and signalled her to come down, but she just shook her head and kept on climbing.'

He stared ahead blindly, reliving the event.

'She always was so obstinate. There was nothing I could do to force her to come back, she was too far away. I just had to watch her until she climbed on out of my sight and then I headed back down the mountain as fast as I could to warn the mountain patrol. By that time, it was snowing heavily and there was zero visibility. They couldn't take the helicopter out until the storm had passed and I just kept praying that she'd find some shelter but — ' His voice broke. 'We didn't find her until three days later. She had fallen down a rock face.'

He looked at Andrea with such unutterable misery that she pushed herself upright and slowly hugged him to her, rocking his body and cradling his head on her shoulder.

'It must have been awful,' she whispered. 'But, Luke, you weren't to blame. You couldn't have stopped her.'

'I should have known she would follow me. If I hadn't been so keen to do that climb she would still be alive.'

'Did you love her?' The question left her lips before she could stop it.

There was a long silence. Luke pulled away from her, running his hand through his hair.

'Love her? Yes, for a while I suppose I did. And I thought she loved me. She was a graphic artist in the New York studio where I worked. She was bright, funny, beautiful. A lot like you.'

Before Andrea could think about the implications of that remark, he continued in a quiet voice.

'She was good, too, in her work. She was a terrific help to me when I first arrived in America — she seemed to know everyone in the advertising world and she introduced me to the right people, took me to all the right places. And then there was her love of climbing. I'd never met a girl who was so keen to do top-grade rock climbing. She was an odd mixture of party girl and sportswoman and whatever she did, she gave it all she'd got. I suppose that's what attracted me to her in the first place. Hailey was really enthusiastic about everything she did. I'd never known anyone like her.'

'What went wrong?'

'At first, it was just a lot of little things. Hailey really loved to party, and to please her, I'd go along, too. But working all day and partying all night — that's never been my idea of a life. Then I found out that she was incredibly ambitious, and that she wasn't averse to stabbing people in the back to get where she wanted to be. All the studios where she'd worked in the past were full of people who hated her for what she'd done to them on the way up. Then she — ' He stopped. 'I don't know why I'm telling you all this. It's history.'

'Go on,' she urged.

'She did it to me.'

'What, stabbed you in the back?'

'Not literally. But she knew all about an ad campaign that I was working on; I'd never had any secrets from her — she was in the same studio for heavens sake! She took the whole concept with her to another agency and got a job there on the strength of it.'

Andrea was shocked. 'How could she take your idea?'

'Easily, really. The campaign I was working on was a long-term thing. It wasn't due to hit the media for another couple of months. She sold the idea to a rival agency for a product that wanted a new campaign immediately. They had the whole thing in the national papers and on TV before I'd even shown my ideas to the client. A month's work down the drain.'

'What did you do about it? Couldn't you sue her or something?'

He laughed harshly. 'It wasn't worth it. I did something better in the end anyway. But that little career move of hers was the end of us. Not that there had ever been any real commitment from either of us anyway.'

'And after that you still went climbing with her?'

'Good lord, no. After she pulled that little trick, I could hardly bring myself to speak to her. But that weekend she called me and said she wanted to see me, to clear things up between us. When I told her I wasn't interested in having a long talk about a relationship that, as far as I was concerned, had never meant anything anyway, she started begging me to take her up the mountain. She probably thought that if we climbed together we'd get close again. All our best times together had been on the mountain, you see. That's half the reason I told her she couldn't come with me.'

He turned to Andrea and cupped her chin in his hand.

'That's enough of that particular bedtime story,' he said decisively. 'You need some sleep. Doctor's orders.'

She held his gaze. 'So do you think I'm going to stab you in the back some day soon?'

'What? Why do you say that?'

'You said I'm a lot like her.'

His puzzled look turned to one of amusement.

'I said you were bright, funny and

beautiful. But other than that, you're not a bit like Hailey.'

His eyes never left hers and she held her breath, afraid to break the intensity of the moment.

Slowly he gathered her into his arms and kissed her tenderly. Somehow his lips stayed where they were, and his arms tightened about her, drawing her closer and closer, fusing her soft contours with his. All thoughts of the pain in her limbs were drowned in a flood of overwhelming sensations.

'Andrea, my love,' he muttered huskily.

Then abruptly he pulled away and almost angrily jerked the blanket back to cover her shoulders.

His breath came in gasps, his eyes dark with passion.

He stood up and switched off the bedside light.

'We'll talk in the morning.' He squeezed her hand. 'Sleep well.'

★　★　★

The next morning, Andrea awoke surprisingly refreshed, and immediately memories of the previous evening came flooding back to her.

She lay in a contented daze reliving Luke's caresses, and wondered if he would come through to wake her or if he would let her get up in her own time.

She got out of bed slowly, and suddenly remembered that although the shirt of Luke's that she had slept in would have doubled as a mini, it was all she had to wear. But she needn't have worried. Her own clothes, now dry, were folded on a chair beside the bed.

She picked them up and found the bathroom without difficulty.

Emerging full of renewed energy and in glowing spirits, Andrea felt that the bowl of soup from the night before had been eaten a long time ago. Her thoughts turned urgently to breakfast, but the house around her was strangely silent. Could Luke still be asleep?

Downstairs, Jessie greeted her with a

feathery salute of her tail, but she didn't get up from her big basket in the corner of the kitchen.

The kitchen showed no sign of anyone having eaten breakfast there that morning and, peering out of the window, Andrea noticed that the camper van was not parked in its usual place at the gate. Odd, she thought. Perhaps he's gone out to buy the Sunday papers.

Then she noticed that an envelope addressed to her had been stuck to the door of the fridge, and she tore it open.

The message inside could not have been more terse.

'8 a.m. Gone to sort out trouble at studio. Make yourself breakfast then call a taxi to take you home. Luke.'

There was a five-pound note pinned to the paper.

Puzzled, she re-read the note. What was the trouble at the studio? And why was the whole tone of the note so cold?

Suddenly she didn't feel hungry any more; all she wanted was to get back to her own flat.

She went through to the front room to phone for a taxi, slammed the door behind her and waited on the pavement until it arrived.

* * *

For the rest of the day, Andrea sat alone, nursing her wounds both physical and mental. Her body ached all over and she was covered in small bruises on her arms and legs.

She made herself a big pot of tea and curled up in her armchair overlooking the park, going over the past twenty-four hours.

Did Luke regret allowing her to get so close to him the previous evening? Was this his way of saying that it meant nothing, that they were back to their old businesslike relationship? Surely he can't think that I can just forget last night, she thought angrily. Did it really all mean nothing to him?

She was certain of one thing. Things between her and Luke had moved on to a completely different footing. His kisses of the previous evening and the intimate feelings he had shared with her meant that things could never be the same between them.

She fully expected that Grant would phone her during the morning, or even come around to her flat without warning, as he often did. But the phone remained silent and there was no sign of the little green sports car outside.

Filled with sudden resolve, she picked up the phone and dialled Grant's number, determined to invite him round and to tell him that their relationship was over. She couldn't put it off any longer, much as she wanted to avoid the scene she knew would follow her announcement.

While she waited for him to pick up the receiver, she rehearsed in her mind what she would say — 'My feelings have changed . . . it's not fair to you . . . always be the best of friends.' But even as she thought them, the words rang hollow.

She wished she had the courage to just tell him the truth. She wished she could say, 'Grant, you've never really loved me, you've only loved the idea of having a willing idiot at your beck and call. And I was happy to be that willing idiot. But not any more, not now that I've found what real love feels like.'

She let the phone ring several times before she gave up, wondering where he could be. His Sunday morning routine, for the past three months at least, had been to sleep late then call for her and take her out for a long lunch somewhere, followed by a film and later another meal or a snack at a jazz club.

Ever since she'd met him, her weekends had been tailored to his wishes, and she had put off scores of invitations so that she was available to do whatever he decided they'd do.

But that will all change now, she thought with satisfaction. I'll be doing a lot more mountain walks with Luke, for one thing . . .

Thinking of Luke brought back the

anxiety she felt about his note, and she phoned the studio number, hoping to get an answer to the riddle.

There was no reply and she pictured the phone ringing in the empty, silent studio. He must be back home already, she thought, and dialled the number of his house.

Still no reply.

Andrea grew more and more uneasy. What could this trouble possibly be? Had he discovered a mistake in an advertisement, something for which she was responsible?

She racked her brains but could think of nothing that could have caused him to rush out of his house on a Sunday morning the way he had.

Maybe there was a typographic error with something of Jeannie's, she thought, feeling immediately guilty at her faint hope that it was Jeannie's mistake and not her own that had caused the fuss.

Unable to settle or relax, she paced around her flat, picking things up and putting them down again. She wished she could go out for a breath of fresh air, but the steady drip of rain outside her window discouraged her.

She felt a desperate need to talk to someone — anyone. Of course — Barbara. She'd tell Barbara of her adventures on Forris Crag; at least *she* was always ready for a chat. And Andrea would tell her that she was about to break up with Grant, so the field would be clear for the other girl.

But Barbara's phone, too, rang and rang and rang without being answered.

★ ★ ★

Gosh, Andrea, you don't look so good this morning. Heavy weekend, was it?'

Stephanie's cheerful greeting did nothing to make her feel any better. Andrea had dragged herself off to the studio, still aching in every joint and with her body feeling bruised and battered all over.

She would happily have stayed at home but for her anxiety about Luke's mysterious disappearance the day before.

Feeling extremely fragile, she limped towards the studio, wondering how she was going to be able to throw herself into the Spectrum computer campaign with the enthusiasm that was required.

Perhaps she'd be able to go home at lunch-time and sleep for the rest of the day; she was sure Luke would understand.

Luke's leather jacket was hanging on its peg and without even stopping at her own desk, she walked through to his office, knocking briefly on his door.

'Hi!'

The smile died on her lips as he looked up with an expression that frightened her. His face was carved in granite and his eyes were dark with anger.

'Please come in and close the door behind you.'

Startled, she did so.

'I'm glad you came in early.'

There was a quiet menace in his tone and he made no enquiries as to her condition after her fall.

'I'd like your comments on these, please.'

He pushed a pile of photocopied drawings towards her. With a shock of recognition, Andrea looked at what appeared to be rough layouts for several advertisements. They all featured babies in business suits. One of them was drawn with outsized horn-rimmed spectacles and was waving a handful of pamphlets on which were printed the words *'Banking Rates'*.

Her horrified eyes travelled to the caption, *'It's Fastabank for the men of the future'*.

'But how . . . ?'

'Do you see the name of the advertising agency?'

Her eyes dropped to the logo, *'Another great campaign from the studios of Mattler Horne'*, stamped on the corner of each photocopy. Mattler Horne!

As the implications of this hit her, her knees turned to jelly and she sank into the chair opposite Luke, feeling ill.

Fastabank — Grant's account.

The frigid silence lengthened as she tried numbly to think of a reasonable explanation. How was it possible for Mattler Horne to be planning advertisements almost identical to the one's she'd prepared for United Northern?

'I'm waiting to hear your thoughts on the matter.'

Luke's words fell like stones of ice into the silent chasm between them.

'I'd especially like you to explain how it happens to be Mattler Horne that is responsible for this.'

Transfixed by his rage, Andrea could only stare at him.

'It — it must be some sort of coincidence,' she whispered.

Even as she said the words she was aware of how silly they sounded.

'Coincidence? I think not. It seems to me quite obvious what has happened.'

She drew back at the savage contempt in his voice which was all the more frightening because it he hadn't raised it above more than a whisper.

'It seems to me that you told your friend Grant Carter all about our plans for United Northern, and he fed them to the art director of Mattler Horne as his own ideas.'

She found her voice with difficulty.

'No, I didn't. I didn't tell Grant anything about the campaign. I never mentioned it to him after you told us not to.'

He snorted in disbelief. 'I suppose I can hardly expect you to admit it. But unless you can come up with some plausible way in which Mattler Horne could have found out about what we were doing, I can only assume that I am correct. You were simply unable to stop yourself talking about our confidential business. For all I know, you might even have shown him the photographs we used. It certainly looks like it.'

'Luke, please — I give you my word of honour that I never breathed a word to Grant about the United Northern campaign.'

He narrowed his eyes. 'Your word of

honour? But how much is your word of honour worth? I wonder if you even know the meaning of the word?'

'Luke, there has to be another explanation.'

She cast her thoughts around wildly.

'Maybe they broke into Joe's studio and saw the photographs there? Maybe someone from the casting agency told them we were using toddlers and they guessed the rest . . . ' Her voice trailed off into silence. 'But how did you get hold of those layouts?' she asked him. 'How did you find out they were preparing the same campaign?'

'Now that *was* pure coincidence. Joe went back to the tailor on Saturday to ask him for another little suit — one of ours got damaged and he needed to shoot some more pics. The tailor mentioned that someone from Mattler Horne had been into his shop and had ordered three identical little suits. It wasn't difficult to guess the rest.'

'What are you going to do? Our campaign's ready to start next week.'

'Luckily I was able get hold of their art director yesterday and I've stopped their campaign from going ahead. I was able to prove we'd been working on ours for weeks and I threatened legal action. The guy was horrified. He admitted the idea had come from one of their account executives but he wouldn't say who.'

'And you're sure it was Grant?'

'People in love do very stupid things, and I'm afraid you, Andrea, have done something unbelievably stupid. And in the end it did neither of you any good, since your precious Grant Carter was fired from Mattler Horne anyway. Even using you to help him with his underhand way of doing things couldn't save his job.'

Stunned at his words, she could do nothing but stare at him while hot tears welled up and ran unchecked down her cheeks.

'You've got to believe me! This had nothing to do with — with what there used to be between me and Grant. I want to sort this out as much as you do!'

' 'What used to be between you'?' His voice echoed his disbelief. 'The last I heard, you were going to marry him as soon as it could be arranged. Although I must say, after Saturday night, I have to wonder if you are as ready for marriage to him as you claim.'

This cutting reference to what had passed between them was like a hammer blow. How could a man, one as open and tender as Luke had been to her after her fall, change so completely? How could he even think she'd be such a traitor to him and to her work? He had condemned her without listening to a word she'd said.

A furious rage bubbled up within her and exploded.

'I am not in love with Grant and I am not going to marry him. I did not tell Grant anything about our work here. But if you've decided — without bothering to look any further — that I'm to blame for this mess, then all I can say is that I don't want to work for someone who doesn't trust me in any case. I resign and I'm leaving right now.'

Trembling and biting back tears, she stood up and turned to leave the room, but Luke, equally angry, leapt to his feet and gripped her arm.

'I don't accept your resignation!' he yelled at her. 'You'll stay until I get to the bottom of this story. If you think you can just escape the consequences of your actions by running away like — like — '

'Like Hailey?' Andrea lifted her chin and looked at him scornfully. 'That's the whole problem, isn't it? You're thinking of Hailey and what she did to you.

'Well, I'm not Hailey, but you haven't realised that. You just think every woman you meet is either going to fall into your arms or stab you in the back. Well, I'm not going to do either. But what I *am* going to do is get to the truth of this thing and when I do, you can apologise. And after that, you can accept my resignation. Now let me go!'

She wrenched herself free of his grasp and walked out of his office with as much dignity as she could muster before huge sobs shook her body.

Andrea Takes the Blame

Jeannie was sitting stiffly at her desk pretending to work, but she swung around when she heard Luke's door open.

'What's going on?' she hissed. 'I've never heard such a row!' Then she saw Andrea's tears and rushed to put her arms around the older girl. 'Oh, Andy, don't cry! It can't be as bad as all that! Don't let Luke get to you like this.'

Jeannie hugged her close and Andrea allowed herself the luxury of burying her head in her shoulder and letting the tears flow. Darn it, she thought angrily, if he comes through into the studio and sees me like this he'll think it's a sign of guilt.

She raised her head and wiped her eyes.

'Sorry.' She smiled shakily. 'It's not only that scene with Luke. I was feeling pretty low before I even got here this morning and I guess this was just the last straw.'

'But what was it all about?' Jeannie was agog. 'Stephanie told me she thinks Luke was here all night, and he's had Martin in his office already. What can have happened?'

Before she could answer, Luke wrenched open the door of his office and strode past them, totally ignoring Andrea.

'Jeannie,' he snapped, 'I'll be out all morning with Martin at a photo shoot. Deal with any calls.'

'Me?' Jeannie's voice rose to a squeak. But he was out of the studio before she could finish her protests.

Andrea looked at her.

'I'm not exactly the flavour of the month around here today,' she said dryly. 'Maybe he's trying you out as his new assistant.'

'Me?' Jeannie squeaked again, turning to Andrea with such a look of horror that she couldn't help smiling.

She told Jeannie briefly what had been said in Luke's office that morning. Watching her doubtful face as she listened made it clear to Andrea that Jeannie had come to the same conclusion as Luke, although she was too tactful to come right out and say it.

'Are you sure you didn't take some work home and maybe Grant took a peek at it?'

'I'm absolutely sure that didn't happen, Jeannie.'

She noticed dully that even she herself wasn't arguing any more with the fact that somehow it had been Grant who had supplied the ideas to Mattler Horne.

She knew Jeannie was longing for a lot more discussion on the subject, but she felt drained and exhausted.

'Leave it, Jeannie. I just don't feel like talking about it any more.'

Andrea went slowly to hang up her coat, wondering what to do next. She knew she had to confront Grant as soon as she could — not only to break off their relationship but also to tackle him about the leak of the United Northern campaign. But she dreaded the scene that would follow. What a fool I was not to break off with him properly last week and get it over with, she thought.

Sitting in front of her computer, she stared blankly at the screen without switching it on.

Finishing the artwork for the Spectrum campaign was top priority, but what should she do? In his rage, Luke hadn't mentioned it and she wasn't even sure if she would be allowed to continue working on it.

There was a pile of smaller jobs waiting for attention but she could hardly lift her arms to the keyboard. A headache started throbbing behind her eyes and her whole body felt stiff and sore. This is ridiculous, she thought. I'm wasting time and I'm not getting anything done. I'm going home to bed. I wish I'd never come in.

She stood up abruptly. 'Jeannie, I feel as though I'm coming down with flu. I think I'll just — '

But as she spoke the telephone on her desk buzzed. It was Grant.

'Andy, where have you been hiding? I tried to reach you on Friday and again the whole of Saturday. Where on earth have you been?' His voice was indignant. 'I wanted to go to that new place on Fraser Street for supper and you were nowhere to be found.'

'Sorry, Grant, I should have phoned you, I know.' She found herself apologising before she could stop herself. 'Listen, I need to speak to you. Can we meet for lunch?'

'What, today? Well, as you obviously haven't remembered, I started here at Atherstone's today. I'm phoning you from my new office — which, by the way, is a very nice size. I've got a good view of the river and it's right on the corner, next to the Director's.' His voice was smug. 'At least they seem to know how to treat their account executives here. But I don't know if I can get away for lunch just like that; I'll have to see what the routine is around here. Maybe I'll be expected to lunch with the rest of the executives.'

'Grant, it's important. I must see you. Today.'

'What's the rush? Can't it keep until tonight?'

'No. Meet me in the park at one o'clock — I'll wait for you there at the fountain.'

She put down the phone before he could argue, and looked across at Jeannie who was unashamedly listening to every word.

'Now we'll find out the truth,' Andrea said, and went through to Luke's office.

The rough layouts from Mattler Horne were still lying on his desk and she picked one up and put it in her bag.

*   *   *

'This had better be important, Andy. I was invited to join the other guys for lunch but I had to refuse and it didn't look good. I mean, I need to meet everyone socially to see where they fit in and so on.' Grant thrust his hands in to his pockets impatiently. 'What's this all about? And why weren't you answering your phone over the weekend?'

Andrea wet her lips and wordlessly showed him the layout, never taking her eyes from his face. In one instant she read the guilt that flashed across his face as he looked at it.

'And? What's the problem?'

So, he was going to try to bluster this out.

'This has been produced by Mattler Horne,' she said quietly.

'I can see that. Fastabank is one of my — or should I say, *was* one of my biggest accounts there. Now I'm with Atherstone's, of course, but Fastabank are still my clients.'

She nodded. 'I need to know how Mattler Horne came up with this idea for an advertisement — an idea which is exactly like the one that Market Media are running for United National in a couple of weeks.'

'Is it? Well, it must be a coincidence,' he said coolly. 'But I don't know what it's got to do with me. Don't forget, I'm an account executive, not an art director. Ideas for campaigns aren't my line, Pumpkin, but I imagine that using babies in an advertisement isn't exactly a new idea.'

'Don't call me Pumpkin. I hate that name. And using babies in a financial advertisement like this, with a caption which is almost exactly the same, is too much of a coincidence to *be* a coincidence. And the art director at Mattler Horne told Luke that one of the account executives gave him the idea.'

'And just who do you think that was?' asked Grant, his face cold and without expression. 'It sounds as if you're pointing the finger at me.'

'Oh, Grant, don't play games and don't lie to me,' she cried angrily. 'I don't know how you did it, but you managed to find out about our campaign and sell the idea to Fasta-bank.'

'That's ridiculous. Why should I bother to do that?' He sounded bewildered by her attack. 'The Mattler Horne art director was quite able to think up his own ideas. And how was I supposed to find out about it anyway? You never discuss your work with me any more, you're like a clam.'

'I know I didn't tell you anything, but you found out somehow,' she said stubbornly. 'It had to be you, Grant, you're the only connection between our studio and Mattler Horne.'

'Sorry, sweetie, not guilty,' he said cheerfully. 'If your campaign was something like this, then it's just bad luck. This idea was kicking around our studio weeks ago, but I assure you, I had nothing to do with it. Actually,' he looked at the layout critically, 'it's rather good, don't you think?'

His tone was so casual that Andrea would have doubted his connection with the advertisement if she hadn't seen his expression when she'd first shown it to him.

'Yes, it is good,' she said slowly. 'It's so good that you stole it and used it. No matter how much you deny it, I know it was you. I just need to know how.'

'Andy, my sweetie, what's got into you?' Grant moved closer and tried to put his arm around her shoulders.

'Stop it, Grant, it's over. You and me. I don't want to see you any more.'

The words came out easily and she felt nothing but a deep regret that she'd taken so long to say them. She'd gone over this scene so often in her mind, always imagining that she'd be choking with tears or that she'd stumble over the words. But it was easy.

'Oh, come now! You're just upset about this silly business; you don't mean that.' He glared at her impatiently. 'The trouble with you, Andrea, is that you take your job far too seriously. It's only an advertisement, for heaven's sake. It's not the end of the world!'

'It's not just this advert, Grant, it's everything. It's the way you flirt with every girl you meet. It's the way you don't keep your promises. The way you lie to people, even your mother. No, it's over. I don't want to see you ever again.'

'Flirt with every girl I meet?' His tone of injured innocence almost made her laugh out loud. 'I suppose you mean Barbara. It was just a few kisses, Andy, and it didn't mean a thing. I was only trying to be nice to the poor girl, but I suppose the silly little fool told you all about it!'

'You're wrong,' she snapped. 'Barbara hasn't mentioned anything to me about you kissing her. And yes, I know now that your kisses mean nothing — not to you, at any rate. And I have no doubt you can charm almost any girl to do anything you want, Grant, but not me. Not any more. It's over.'

'Well, fine!' He was breathing heavily, a mocking expression on his face. 'It might interest you to know that your so-called best friend was the one who told me all about your wonderful campaign. She can never stop telling me how clever you are. And if you wouldn't tell me what you were up to, she was more than happy to; in fact, she couldn't stop boasting about you to me.'

Andrea swallowed. Barbara would never be that indiscreet. Would she?

'You're wrong,' she said with conviction. 'Barbara wouldn't discuss my work with you. She knows how much that campaign means to me. She knew everything I told her was in confidence.'

'The stupid woman's in love with me — why shouldn't she tell me what I wanted to know?' he jeered. 'She knew I needed to come up with something for the Fastabank campaign. Why do you think they agreed to stick with me when I left Mattler Horne? They loved this idea and they knew it was mine.'

'Yours?'

He had the grace to look a little ashamed.

She shook her head wearily. It didn't seem to matter any more. 'Poor Grant. I'm really sorry for you.'

'Sorry for me?' He laughed derisively, his handsome features twisted into an ugly expression. 'You? You haven't a clue about anything, and you're sorry for me? Look at the way you live! Look at the way you dress! You have absolutely no class! Mother had it exactly right when she said you weren't quite from the top drawer, didn't she?'

'Class!' She choked with rage. 'When you finally find out the meaning of that word, Grant, don't bother to let me know.'

She turned on her heel and walked away towards the bus stop. It was time to talk to Barbara.

★   ★   ★

Standing outside Barbara's flat, biting her lip with impatience, she thought at first that there was no one at home. Her second knock, however, brought a soft response from behind the door.

'Who's there?'

'It's me, Andrea.'

She heard the sound of the key in the lock and the door opened slowly.

Andrea was shocked to see her friend's face red and swollen with crying.

'Oh, Andy, I'm so glad you've come!' Barbara flung her arms around her neck and hugged her tightly. 'I've been trying to reach you at the studio all morning but they said you'd gone home, and then I couldn't get you there either.'

'Barbs, what's the matter? Why the tears?'

Her friend's distraught face wiped all her own problems from her mind. She led her to the sofa and said comfortingly, 'Tell me what's happened. And please don't cry, I can't bear to see you so unhappy.'

Slowly, between sobs, the story came out.

'Last Saturday evening Grant came

round and invited me out to dinner. He said you were working right through the weekend and that he was lonely. So I went along with him to that fancy place that's just opened — oh, Andy, I wish I hadn't! How could I have been so stupid? But we had a really nice time and then he came back here for coffee and then he — I think I'd had too much to drink — '

'Barbs, honestly, a few kisses really don't matter to me,' Andrea interrupted gently. 'Grant and I are finished anyway.'

'No, it *does* matter,' Barbara insisted tearfully. 'You're my best friend and I let myself get involved with your fiancé! I can't forgive myself, Andy, and I can't expect you to either. I'm just so ashamed. The last thing I want to do is cause trouble between you and Grant; I know how much you love him. But I had to get it off my chest and tell you, or I'd never be able to live with myself.'

'Listen, Barbara.' Andrea took her friend's hand in her own. 'Grant's not my fiancé and never has been. I've known for a long time that he's not the right man for me, and for the whole of last week I was trying to summon up the courage to tell him so. Now those Fastabank adverts have just brought things to a head and we've broken up completely. It had absolutely nothing to do with anything going on between you and Grant.'

'What Fastabank advertisement? What are you talking about?' Barbara was puzzled. 'I thought your big client was called United Northern?'

Andrea took a deep breath. 'Grant accused you of something and I need to know if it's true. Did you ever discuss my United Northern campaign with him? The adverts with the babies?'

'Of course I didn't.' Barbara's denial was emphatic. 'Good heavens, he was with a rival agency; I would never have said a thing. Why do you ask?'

Andrea explained about the rough layouts that Luke had shown her.

'While he was with Mattler Horne,

Grant's biggest client was Fastabank. And these roughs are almost identical to the ones I designed for United Northern. They all have babies wearing suits and the caption is almost word for word what I had before Luke changed it. Theirs read, '*It's Fastabank for the men of the future*', and my caption was, '*Men of the future use United Northern*'. Then Luke suggested, '*Tomorrow's men use United Northern today*', so we used that caption in the finished work. Somehow, Grant found out the theme of our campaign and pinched the idea.'

'Did Grant ever go into your studio? I thought Luke had forbidden anyone but you artists to go in there,' asked Barbara.

'No, I'm positive he never once came into the studio after Luke took over as art director. But Luke won't believe me when I say I don't know how Grant could have got hold of the idea, and now Grant's claiming that you gave him all the details.'

Barbara was horrified. 'What? I

certainly did not! How dare he say such a thing? Actually, Grant was always asking me about your work — remember, I mentioned that he was always talking about you and what you were doing. I often had to tell him I knew nothing about the jobs you were working on. I thought it was a bit odd that he kept coming back to the subject of your work all the time.'

'Mmm. Well, now I guess we know why.'

Andrea was hugely relieved to hear Barbara's denial, but the fact remained that Grant had found out about her ideas for the campaign somehow.

'Did you ever leave anything lying around your flat that he might have seen? Some rough notes or anything?' Barbara asked.

Andrea thought back and shook her head. 'No, never. I was terribly careful. Luke's paranoid about secrecy.'

Even as she said this, she gave an involuntarily gasp as a picture popped into her mind of a folder she'd taken from the studio to work on one night. She'd left it in Barbara's flat and, up to now, had completely forgotten about it.

'Barbs, did you ever find a folder I left here — oh, weeks ago? I remember I meant to work on it at home but then found I'd left it here.'

'Why, yes, I did.' Barbara stiffened. 'I gave it to Grant without thinking. It was the same night you left it on the table by the front door. He said he'd be seeing you the next day and took it when he left. I had no idea what was in it, though. Didn't he return it to you?'

So that was how he had discovered all the details. The folder had been full of copies of the rough layouts for the campaign.

Andrea bit her lip as the full implications of her carelessness hit home. Luke had been right all along. It was through her that Grant had obtained his information. Even if she hadn't told him directly, the leak had been her fault and hers alone.

She said good night to Barbara and

slowly made her way home. She wanted nothing more than to crawl into bed, pull the blankets over her head and sleep. She just had to make one phone call first.

With a dry mouth, she dialled the number of Market Media.

'Stephanie? Is Luke there, please?'

'No, he's not. Andrea, where are you? Jeannie said you'd had a huge row with Luke and he went off looking like a thundercloud. What's going on between you two?'

'Nothing. Just put me through to Jeannie in the studio,' she said curtly.

Jeannie's nervous greeting changed to relief when she realised that it was Andrea on the line and not a client.

'Andy, how are you? Are you feeling better? Did you speak to Grant?'

'Yes. Listen, Jeannie, I must get a message to Luke as soon as possible. Have you any idea where he is?'

'As far as I know he's at Joe's video studio.'

'Right. Tell him it *was* Grant who

stole our idea. And tell him it was *my* fault because I left some work where he could see it. And tell him I resign. My letter of resignation will be in the post tomorrow.'

Jeannie's protests and questions sounded in her ears as she gently replaced the receiver. Then she unplugged the telephone, drew the curtains, and allowed her bruised and aching body to relax in the warmth of her bed. But as she lay waiting for the merciful oblivion of sleep, she knew there was nothing she could do to soothe the ache in her heart.

* * *

'Aren't these beans wonderful?' Scraping the wet mud from her shoes before she entered her mother's kitchen, Andrea showed off the home-grown vegetables with delight. 'It's so lovely having a big garden like yours, Mum; one day I'm going to have one just the same.'

'Are you, my lovie? That's nice.' Mrs Ross smiled at her youngest child with undisguised pleasure. 'Let's give them a bit of a rinse then, and we'll have them with our supper tonight.'

Since her daughter's unexpected arrival two days earlier, Mrs Ross had enjoyed having her around as she went about her daily tasks. But quite why Andy had suddenly appeared on the doorstep with only a few hours' warning, or why she'd chosen to spend her annual leave at home, helping her mother around the house and taking the dogs for long lonely walks on the hills, she didn't know. But as soon as she'd seen her daughter walking up the path with her rucksack on her back and her face white and miserable, her mother's instinct had told her that there was trouble somewhere. Mrs Ross had no doubt that Andy would tell her when she was ready, but until then she wisely kept her own counsel.

Now Andrea stood at the sink and ran some water over the beans, looking out of the window as she did so. Her mother's garden rambled down to a low stone wall and beyond that she could see the mist swirling down from the purple hills which rose beyond the edge of the village.

'I'd forgotten how beautiful it all is here. I've been away too long.' She gave her mother a wistful grin. 'It's a pity there isn't an advertising studio in Lannock. I'd love to stay around here for a while; it's so peaceful.'

'I'd give you two weeks before you'd be chafing to be off again,' said her mother, smiling. 'I remember you were always hankering after the bright lights. Had enough of them, then?'

'I think so.' Andrea sighed. 'I need a change, Mum. I'm tired of my job and it's high time I took off and saw something of the world. Africa, maybe. Or Australia.' Anywhere but back to Lymchester.

Her mother looked at her shrewdly. 'Do you feel you need a change because you're tired or because of something that happened down south?'

'Both, really.'

313

'Something did happen, then?'

Andrea caught her bright and interested eye.

'Oh, Mum, it was nothing. Everyone needs a change of scene. I've been working there for three years!'

'And what about that Grant Carter? Are you two still going out?'

For months, Andrea's letters had been full of this man Grant but since she'd been home she hadn't mentioned his name once.

'No, that's all over.'

Her bleak voice warned Mrs Ross that it was time to change the subject.

'How about a game of Scrabble before tea?' she suggested and the next hour was spent in cheerful combat over the board.

Later, when her mother went through to the kitchen to prepare the evening meal, Andrea opened the front door and looked out at the clouds that were gradually sinking lower and lower. She reached for her waterproof jacket and shrugged it on, suddenly needing the freedom of a lone walk on the hills before dark.

Her mother's two golden Labradors pushed at her with their wet noses and whined with excitement.

'Come on, boys,' she said and they rushed past her and out of the door, tails waving like flags. 'Just off for a bit of fresh air, Mum,' she called. 'I won't be long.'

Andrea had posted her letter of resignation the day after she'd spoken to Jeannie. Without waiting for Luke's reaction to her message, that same afternoon she'd packed some clothes, locked up her flat, and caught the train to Scotland.

As the train had eaten up the miles towards her home, she'd been guiltily aware that she was running away from Luke, running away from *everything*, and that she was leaving a lot of unfinished business behind her.

But he called me a liar, she'd thought miserably, remembering the icy look of scorn in his eyes. Whatever she'd imagined there had been between herself and Luke had withered and died.

Like a wounded animal, all she'd wanted to do was crawl into a hole and lick her wounds, and so she'd headed for her childhood home and for the comfort of her mother's arms.

* * *

She'd been feeling hollow and depressed all morning but her mood improved as she walked up the hill, with the fresh sweet smell of heather filling her lungs and the cool evening air on her face. This was a time to plan a new beginning — a complete change of scene, as far away from Luke as possible so that eventually she would be able to erase the memory of him from her mind.

She'd see a travel agent as soon as she could and enquire about air fares to Australia. Maybe she could find an advertising job in Sydney or Melbourne. But to do this, she'd need to show them a portfolio of her published work. She grimaced. So there was no way she could avoid going back to the studio. She'd have to retrieve her copies of all the layouts she'd done in the past.

Somehow, in her mad flight from Lymchester, Andrea had imagined she could just resign and that would be the end of it. No need to see Luke again. She'd had several weeks' leave owing to her, so she'd felt she could walk out with a clear conscience. But she hadn't bargained on the sleepless nights when visions of Luke relentlessly swirled through her mind and hot waves of longing for him swept through her body.

I've handled everything so badly, she thought. Why didn't I admit to myself what I was feeling about Luke from almost the minute I met him? Why did I go on fooling myself about Grant? If I'd been honest with myself, none of this would have happened. Now I'll never see Luke again.

And as for a clear conscience, when she thought about the Spectrum campaign she felt an overwhelming sense of remorse. The three-week deadline had been tight enough with two of them working on it — how would Luke manage on his own?

Very well, probably, she thought wryly, without me to argue with him all the time. I'm not indispensable. But she missed the buzz of the studio and the easy camaraderie.

Her mother had been right — she couldn't stand the peace and quiet of the village for much longer. She decided that she would stay for the rest of the week and then she would go back to Lymchester, pack up properly, sublet her flat, and set off to see the world.

A fine rain began to fall, and the mist started to curl up the valley. She turned reluctantly for home, whistling the dogs to her side. They returned, wet and muddy and panting, to lead the way down the path.

Andrea followed them, lost in thought. However, her reverie was broken by a soft growl. Both dogs had come to a halt, ears pointing into the mist, tails rigid, as they listened to something moving on the path ahead of them.

'What is it, boys?' Andrea could hear nothing but the wind blowing across the grass and the drip of rain off her parka. Then the ghostly shape of a huge animal appeared out of the mist and she gave a small scream of fright before she recognised it as Jessie.

Before Andrea had understood what was happening, Luke was there, too; standing in front of her, barring her way.

For a long moment they gazed into each other's eyes. Then, with a strangled moan, he swept her into his arms, crushing her body to his, his lips hungrily seeking hers in greedy, compulsive kisses.

Her senses spun as she clung to him; her body moulded to his as she responded joyfully to his embrace. This is a dream, she thought hazily, and I don't want to wake up. But Luke's solid presence was real enough.

'You little idiot, did you think I wouldn't find you?' His voice was husky with emotion. 'What possessed you to run off like that?'

Safe in the comfort of his arms, with her face pressed into his neck, she could only murmur, 'I don't know.'

But she did know that hot tears were coursing down her face to mingle with the rain.

'I've had the devil's own job tracking you down. Don't ever do that again, don't ever leave me!'

'I won't,' she promised, clinging to him tightly.

Some time later she raised her head. 'Did you get my message about the campaign? I told Jeannie . . . '

'Yes. Ssssh.' He placed his finger on her lips. 'Later.'

★　★　★

'Luke, who's Rosalind Kent?' Andrea was snuggled up next to him on her mother's sofa, in front of a blazing fire, with three wet dogs steaming gently on the rug at their feet. Her usually efficient mother was in the kitchen making tea for them all and seemed to be taking a very long time about it.

'Good heavens, what made you think of Rosalind? She's my sister.'

In her wildest dreams Andrea would never have guessed at that. The cool, sophisticated Rosalind Kent might have been his girlfriend, his mistress, even his ex-wife, but never his sister.

'I told you that I came from around Lymchester originally, didn't I?' he continued. 'Rosalind's seven years older than I am. Her husband, Graham, died a year ago and that's one of the reasons I chose to go back there, to see more of her. She's still trying to sort out Graham's estate and I'm giving her a hand.'

Andrea felt a bit of a fool but couldn't resist her next question. 'And who's Penelope?

'The only Penelope I know is my dentist's receptionist. I'm in her bad books because I've cancelled so many appointments lately.' He tipped her face towards his. 'What's this inquisition all about?'

Andrea started to giggle helplessly. 'All these women in your life,' she gasped. 'I was so jealous!'

'Oh, well, if you'd asked me about Sharon or Maureen or Chantal or Elizabeth or — anyway, while we're on the subject of jealously, what about Grant?'

'Grant's history. It was over between us for ages but I just didn't want to admit it to myself or to anyone else. And then I discovered that he'd stolen a folder full of my ideas that I'd left at a mutual friend's flat.'

'I know all the about the folder.'

'You do? How?'

'Your good friend Barbara phoned me a couple of minutes after you'd been to see her on Monday. She couldn't stand the idea of you being wrongly accused by me, the monster of Market Media. She sorted me out in no uncertain terms. She more or less told me that I owe you an apology for doubting your word — and I do.'

'Only half an apology. It was my carelessness that let Grant find out what we were working on.'

'Carelessness, my love, is not what I was accusing you of. I think I went a little bit mad. You were right. When I saw that advertisement it just seemed to be that business with Hailey all over again and I couldn't bear it. I imagined a repeat of the whole scenario, where you were feeding Grant all the details behind my back, and I realised then that I didn't have a chance with you. Can you ever forgive me?'

She answered by raising her face for a kiss which went on and on until they both heard her mother making an elaborate fuss of putting down the tea tray.

They separated quickly, but Luke kept his arm firmly around Andrea's shoulders while he accepted the cup of tea that her mother handed to him.

Mrs Ross looked at the two of them sitting opposite her and smiled to herself. Whatever her daughter's problem had been, it no longer existed, but doubtless it had been something to do with this big fellow with untidy hair who was now wolfing down hot scones and enjoying his third cup of tea. She had a feeling that Andrea wouldn't be staying in Lannock much longer.

'Mrs Ross, these scones are really good. They have a lovely texture. Do you use stoneground flour?'

'Yes, I buy it locally.' She smiled. 'You're a baker, then?'

'Strictly a Sunday baker. A rank amateur compared with you.'

'I can tell a hint when I hear one! Help yourself to another. I'm only too glad to have someone who enjoys his food. Feeding Andy these last couple of days has been like feeding a bird; she's completely lost her appetite.'

Luke looked down at Andrea. 'I think that's a temporary condition,' he said. 'Mrs Ross, how would you feel about having a wedding in your garden?'

'One wedding was quite enough for

me,' she said tartly, 'and I don't accept proposals from men I hardly know.'

Luke gave a great shout of laughter. 'Oh, I'm getting this all wrong. Andrea, will you marry me?'

Trust Luke not to bother with champagne, candlelight and soft music, she thought wryly. Tea and scones and smelly wet dogs instead, for him.

'Luke, my darling, of course I'll marry you,' she said simply.

'And, Mrs Ross, may I have permission to marry your daughter?'

Andrea's mother considered her daughter's face, glowing with quiet happiness. It was the look of a woman who'd found her man.

'Of course,' she said. 'But don't think Andy will keep you in home-made scones. I've never been able to interest her in baking.'

'Then perhaps you could give *me* the recipe for them?'

'Luke! I get the feeling you're marrying me for my mother's cooking!'

'You couldn't be more wrong,' he

whispered, gazing into her eyes.

Unnoticed, her mother diplomatically collected the empty cups and went back to her kitchen, firmly shutting the door behind her.

We do hope that you have enjoyed reading this large print book.

Did you know that all of our titles are available for purchase?

We publish a wide range of high quality large print books including:
Romances, Mysteries, Classics General Fiction Non Fiction and Westerns

Special interest titles available in large print are:
The Little Oxford Dictionary Music Book, Song Book Hymn Book, Service Book

Also available from us courtesy of Oxford University Press:
Young Readers' Dictionary (large print edition) Young Readers' Thesaurus (large print edition)

For further information or a free brochure, please contact us at:
Ulverscroft Large Print Books Ltd., The Green, Bradgate Road, Anstey, Leicester, LE7 7FU, England.
Tel: (00 44) **0116 236 4325**
Fax: (00 44) **0116 234 0205**

WINTER GOLD

Sheila Spencer-Smith

Recovering from a bereavement, Katie Robertson finds an advertisement for a temporary job on the Isles of Scilly that involves looking after a housebound elderly lady for a few weeks. Hoping to investigate a possible family connection, she eagerly applies. But the woman's grandson, Rory, objects to her presence and believes she's involved with sabotaging the family flower farm. With an unlikely attraction growing between them, can Katie's suspicion of the real culprit be proved correct, and lead to happiness?

AFRICAN ADVENTURE

Irena Nieslony

Amateur sleuth Eve Masters has just married the man of her dreams, David Baker, on the romantic island of Crete. Now they are heading off on their honeymoon to Tanzania. Eve has promised her new husband not to get involved in any more mysteries — but when one of their safari party is murdered, she can't help but get drawn in. It isn't long before she's in the middle of a very dangerous game . . .

COULD IT BE MURDER?

Charlotte McFall

Last year's May Day celebrations ended in tragedy for Gemma with the mysterious death of her Aunt Clara. Having inherited her aunt's run-down cottage in her childhood village of Wythorne, Gemma moves in, hoping to investigate the death, and is drawn to Brad, the local pub owner. But what she finds instead is a dead body, and a basket of poisonous mushrooms that have put her unsuspecting friend in hospital. Can Gemma get to the bottom of things before she and Brad become the next victims?